W9-DAW-730

From
Mrs. Geist —

HARPOON

The Story of a Whaling Voyage

A GAM

HARPOON

THE STORY OF A WHALING VOYAGE

FOSTER RHEA DULLES

ILLUSTRATIONS BY CLIFFORD W. ASHLEY

BOSTON · HOUGHTON MIFFLIN COMPANY · NEW YORK

The Riverside Press Cambridge

1935

The Riverside Press

CAMBRIDGE · MASSACHUSETTS

PRINTED IN THE U.S.A.

FOR

MARY RHEA

CONTENTS

ILLUSTRATIONS

I

AT THE CROSSED HARPOONS

David Arrives at 'The Crossed Harpoons'

Chapter I

AT THE CROSSED HARPOONS

FROM within a small, ramshackle frame building, over whose door hung a crudely painted sign with two crossed harpoons, came the sound of singing. At times it could hardly be heard, dying away to a faint murmur, but when the singers swung into the chorus of their song, an overwhelming noise burst forth. The walls of the building shook, while, to the accompaniment of stamping feet and the rattle of ale mugs, a score of throaty voices thundered:

So be cheery, my lads, let your hearts never fail,
While the bold harpooner is striking the whale!

Standing outside in the dark street, David Worth listened eagerly. He had trudged many weary miles along hard-frozen country roads that wintry day in December, 1846, and only his keen desire to ship on a whaling vessel had prevented him many times from turning back to his father's farm. Now that he was in New Bedford, he didn't quite know what to do. He was cold and tired and hungry. The sound of singing, its promise of good cheer, seemed an invitation to end his journey at the sign of the Crossed Harpoons.

For a moment he hesitated. Then, plucking up his courage,

he pushed open the door and stepped from the cold darkness into the pleasant warmth of a well-lighted room.

A crowd of men was lounging about; some of them gathered around an open fire which roared gustily in a great stone fireplace, others seated on benches ranged alongside a heavy wooden table. Their song over, they were talking noisily. Standing in the shadow near the doorway, the boy caught snatches of their conversation.

'Just then he turned on us with a roar like an angry bull and before I could...'

'We went ashore at the Marquesas...'

'"Cut the line!" shouted the Old Man as the whale suddenly...'

At first no one noticed David standing there by the door, his tall, slim figure muffled in a heavy overcoat much too large for him and his knitted cap pulled down well over his head. Nor did he dare to speak to anyone. In all his sixteen years he had never been farther away from the farm than he was at this moment. How could he say anything to these whalemen who had been around Cape Horn, cruised in the Pacific, and fought whales off the shores of distant South Sea islands?

One of the sailors, a great hulk of a man wearing sea boots, dark pantaloons, and a red shirt, whose presence gave off an oily smell as if he had just that day landed after a long voyage, finally caught sight of him.

'Well, my lad,' he sang out in a loud but friendly voice, 'what are you doin' this time of night at the Crossed Harpoons? It looks as if the voyage you'd made was back country somewhere. How are the whales up your way? Better come over here by the fire and get warm.'

Everyone turned to look at the boy as he started across the

room and, confused by the attention he had attracted, he carelessly stumbled against one of the men who was just putting a mug of ale to his mouth. It splashed over his shirt.

'You awkward lout!' the sailor muttered angrily, half rising from the bench. 'I'll teach you...'

'Steady there, old-timer,' quickly shouted the giant who had first greeted David. 'The boy meant no harm. Sit down, lad. You look as if you'd like to get warm and perhaps have a bite to eat. Don't be afraid of a crowd of sailors. Put us in a boat goin' on a whale and we're a pretty fierce lot, but we're ashore now and there ain't nobody more friendly.'

David made his way thankfully to an empty place at the table beside his new friend and soon, feeling much better, was enjoying a mess of bacon and eggs. He had dreamed so often of something like this that it seemed hardly possible that it was really he, David Worth, who was in New Bedford, in an inn called the Crossed Harpoons, sitting down with a group of whalemen. Was he really going whaling? Now that he was here, was he going to be able to find a berth on some vessel bound around Cape Horn? Maybe one of these sailors could tell him what he should do next.

'Mister,' he said, turning to the huge man beside him, 'do you know of any ship which might take me on for a voyage? I know how to work. I'm strong. Why, I can lift old Fanny, our prize sow, and when the colt broke away last spring...'

'Think you can lift a whale, lad? Think, if the mainsail breaks away in a Cape Horn blow, you can hold it down all by yourself? Well, well, well. But what do you want to go whalin' for? It's not much fun out there when a whale busts up your boat, when you're workin' at the try-pots all through a blisterin' hot day and half into the night, when rations run short at sea and there's nothin' to eat but some stale ship biscuit thick with maggots.

'You'd better stay home awhile. Wait a couple of years before you try to sign up for a voyage. You're too young, lad, to ship before the mast on a "blubber-hunter." I don't know why you left home. That's none of my business. But if you'll take my advice, you'll go back. Whalin' ain't the life for a likely-lookin' lad better off at home takin' care of animals than at sea tryin' to kill 'em.'

The sailor said this in a gruff but kindly tone. David could not help feeling that he meant him well. Yet it cast a damper on his enthusiasm just when the warmth of the fire and the reviving effect of his dinner had driven away the doubts and fears which had come over him so often during his long walk to town. If so friendly a person was discouraging about his getting a berth on a whaler, he felt he had little chance of persuading anyone else that he could do his part aboard ship. He was thinking gloomily of the prospect of having to trudge back home and tell his father that his idea of going to sea had all been a mistake, when a commotion broke out on the other side of the room.

'Bet you can't do it, Dago Jack. Bet you two dollars.'

'Here, here's another dollar. It's yours if you do it, on a straight bet.'

'Lay off, Jack. That's no stunt for a whaleman.'

David looked up to see the sailor against whom he had stumbled, the one they called Dago Jack, carefully tying a piece of twine to a fork. What the man was about, he had no idea. Then he noticed another sailor holding a cat, a large gray cat which had been sleeping peacefully before the fire. Everyone was watching the two men.

'It don't count if you just harpoon her,' he heard someone

say. 'The iron's got to hold. If the fork pulls and she gets away, all bets are off. And you got to give the cat a fair chance. Harry has to let her go before you throw.'

Suddenly it dawned on David what they were up to. Dago Jack was going to try to harpoon the cat with the fork and hold her by the string he was tying to the handle. Poor pussy was to be the whale!

The idea sickened him. Why, that cat might just as well be Betsy, the cat back on the farm, his sister's special pet. Hardly knowing what he was doing, David got up and walked over to Dago Jack.

'You can't do that,' he said unsteadily. 'It's cruel.'

The sailor looked up with an angry scowl.

'Who's tellin' me what I can do?' he growled. 'Ready, Harry?'

Dago Jack was smaller than David, a short, stocky Portuguese with a swarthy complexion and beady little eyes beneath thick eyebrows. The boy had hardly noticed him before, and what now caught his attention was an ugly scar which stretched from the corner of one eye almost to his mouth. As his face flushed with anger, this line stood out, a dark, livid streak. For some reason it awakened in David a vague, indistinct memory. He had no time to worry about that, though. Dago Jack was getting up from the bench.

'All right, let her go!' he called.

The sailor called Harry let the cat go. As she started racing across the room, Dago Jack raised his arm to hurl the fork. In a flash David had grabbed his wrist and thrown him back onto the bench. The fork clattered to the floor and the cat escaped through the door leading into the kitchen.

With a startled curse Dago Jack sprang to his feet. Before David knew what had happened, a ringing blow on the side of his head sent the boy reeling against the table.

For a fraction of a second he was stunned. Then his head
cleared quickly. There had been boyhood fights on the
farm; he had been called upon to use his fists before. With
his fighting blood thoroughly aroused, he sailed into Dago
Jack with a cold fury which took the Portuguese completely
by surprise. The whalemen pushed back the table with a
glad shout. Entirely forgetting the cat in this new excitement, they began enthusiastically cheering on the two com-
batants.

A bellow of anger was heard from the corner near the fireplace. In half a dozen gigantic strides, David's first friend
crossed the room. He pushed through the crowd of sailors,
grabbed each of the fighters by the scruff of the neck in one
massive hand, and held them apart as if they had been chil-
dren.

'No more of this!' he thundered.

Then, turning toward the group of sailors:

'A fine bunch of rowdies you are. Fair fight you call it?
You know Dago Jack. What chance has the boy got up
against a fellow who fights like he does? I've seen him draw a
knife in a scrap like this, but he ain't goin' to get a chance to
do anything like that tonight. If anyone's got anything to
say, let him say it.'

As he stood there in the center of the room, still holding the
two fighters apart, the big sailor looked about threateningly.
There were a few subdued growls of protest, but no one dared
to say anything. Finally the sportsmanship of the sailors
asserted itself.

'You're right, Frank,' one of them answered. 'The fight
wouldn't be fair. Dago Jack's a bully and we've had enough
of it. The boy showed a lot of spunk.'

With this, Frank flung Dago Jack back onto the bench, and

letting go his grip on David, walked back to where he had been sitting. The boy followed him, somewhat dazed. What a mess he had got himself into! What might have happened to him had Frank not intervened! As he sat down he ruefully rubbed the side of his head where Dago Jack's ringing blow had landed.

After a few minutes the roomful of sailors had apparently forgotten all about the incident, except for Dago Jack who still slumped morosely in his chair. Someone started up another song. David sat silent and Frank also seemed to be lost in thought.

'Look here,' the latter said unexpectedly when the singing had died down. 'I like your spunk. I've just signed up for another voyage on the Sea Turtle, Captain Obadiah Hunter. She's sailin' tomorrow, for the Pacific. Maybe Captain Hunter can use another green hand. Come down to the docks tomorrow morning, if you still think you want to go whalin'. When you find the Sea Turtle, ask for Frank White. But don't get in any more fights!'

II

THE SEA TURTLE SAILS

David Goes Aboard

Chapter II

THE SEA TURTLE SAILS

THE next morning was bright and clear. After a night at the Crossed Harpoons, where he had been given a small room up under the eaves, David woke up early. At first he could not remember where he was. The room was strange, the view from the window was strange, and the sounds which came up from the street below were very different from the accustomed noises of the farmyard.

Then it all swept over him. He was in New Bedford, he was going down to the docks to hunt for a ship named the Sea Turtle, he was going whaling. He jumped up from his bed and without stopping to close his window, hurried into his clothes and ran downstairs. Should he stop for breakfast? For a moment he thought it would be a foolish waste of time, but then it occurred to him that this Captain Hunter whom he was going to ask for a berth might not want to see him at the crack of dawn. There was really no hurry. He ate a good breakfast, handed over in payment about the last of his carefully hoarded savings, and then set off impatiently for the waterfront.

The sun sparkled on the bay as he walked along the shore and a fresh offshore breeze rippled the surface of the water.

But it was the ships in the harbor which fascinated David. There seemed to be hundreds of them, a forest of wintry masts, tied up to the long docks which lined the waterfront. Some of them looked weather-beaten and worn, as if they had just that day reached port after being badly battered by heavy gales; others were freshly painted and shipshape, ready to start on new voyages. How often had he dreamed of seeing a whaleship, walking its decks, setting forth on a long voyage to far-off seas! He pinched himself to make sure that he was really awake.

Early in the morning as it was, the docks presented a scene of busy activity. At some of them great casks of oil were being swung up out of the ships' holds and trundled along the pier to the warehouses; at others all manner of ship supplies were being unloaded from heavy drays and stored aboard the waiting vessels. Men were at work on many of the whalers, caulking their seams, laying down new planks on the decks, fitting spars, and bending on fresh sails. The sound of the carpenters' and coopers' hammers blended with the rumble of the drays along the cobbled street.

On the stern of every vessel, each one looking almost exactly like its neighbor, was painted its name: the Ocean Rover, the Houqua, the Essex, the Rebecca Sims, the Mystic. David looked eagerly for the Sea Turtle. After some wandering about, he saw a vessel whose decks were so cluttered up with gear that he was sure it must be about to sail, and as he drew near, there, sure enough, was the Sea Turtle.

The boy stopped dead in his tracks and gazed long and hard at the little vessel. As he later learned, she was a 350-ton ship, something over a hundred feet long, twenty-five feet broad, and about thirteen feet deep. Her blunt prow and roomy deck made her appear almost square. He had heard his whaling uncle say whaleships were built by the mile and then sawed off, and looking at the Sea Turtle, it didn't seem impossible. But she had a jaunty air about her for all that, with her bowsprit turned up at a sharp angle and her three masts straight as matchsticks. David noted her after-house, the skids for spare boats, the brick try-works, the whaleboats swung from the heavy wooden cranes set along the bulwarks. He looked up at her mastheads. Would he ever stand there, swaying dizzily as the vessel beneath him pitched and rolled in a heavy sea, watching the horizon for the hazy spot of a distant whale?

It took him some time to get up his courage to go aboard the Sea Turtle. He wished he were older and full grown, a man and not a boy. He rubbed the downy fuzz on his upper lip and tried to imagine what the rough stubble of an unshaved chin must feel like. How could he convince Captain Hunter that he was capable of filling a sailor's berth?

'Well, what do you want?'

David looked up to see a cheerful little man with a thick, black pipe in his mouth leaning against the ship's bulwarks. At first the boy did not know whether he was the person being asked this simple question or not, but no one else was near enough to have heard it, so he concluded he must be.

'Please, sir, is Mr. Frank White aboard?'

The sailor looked at him for a moment, and then without answering turned toward the steerage hatchway and cupping his hands to his mouth shouted in a voice which could have been heard for a quarter of a mile:

'*Mister* Frank White! *Mister* Frank White! A young caller for *Mister* Frank White.'

David felt somewhat abashed by this vehement announcement of his arrival, and was greatly relieved when the bulky form of his friend of the night before emerged from the hatchway.

'Who's doin' all this shoutin' about *Mister* Frank White?' Frank grumbled as he came on deck. 'Somebody goin' to give me command of a ship?' Then he caught sight of the boy standing on the deck and a slow grin spread over his face.

'So you showed up, after all. I thought maybe you'd think better of whalin' when you woke up this morning. Been in any more fights? Jump aboard, jump aboard.'

David sprang up on the bulwarks and for the first time in his life found himself walking the deck of a whaleship.

'Of course I still want to sign up for a voyage,' he said eagerly. 'Do you really think there's any chance aboard the Sea Turtle?'

'I don't know; I don't know,' Frank answered. 'I'm a harpooner, not the captain of this here ship. But I told Captain Hunter a likely looking lad wanted to ship aboard her and you'll have to talk to him. You'll find him in the cabin right now. He's a gruff old fellow, but don't let him frighten you. Speak right up.'

He gave the boy a friendly shove in the direction of the quarterdeck. David walked slowly aft and soon found himself in the cabin standing before a man of about fifty-five, with a thin, lined face framed in graying whiskers. He was bending over some maps spread out on the table in front of him. He did not look up as the boy entered, and paid no attention to him as he stood there nervously twisting his cap in his hands. David didn't quite know what to do, and for what seemed a long time waited for something to happen.

'Well?'

The sharp, sudden question took him by surprise. Captain Hunter had shot a single glance at him from beneath his bushy eyebrows and then turned back to his maps.

'I want to go whaling, sir,' the boy said. 'I'd like to sign aboard the Sea Turtle if you can use another green hand.'

Captain Hunter didn't answer. He ignored the boy completely as he continued to study his maps. David tried again:

'I don't know much about ships, but I'm a good worker. I'm sure I'll learn...'

'What do you want to go to sea for?' Captain Hunter interrupted abruptly.

'I've always wanted to go to sea, sir. My uncle, Captain Bob Worth, told me he'd take me on a voyage...'

'So Captain Bob Worth's your uncle, eh?' Captain Hunter looked the boy over carefully. 'Well, that's a different story. He sailed aboard the Rover, didn't he? And the Rover ain't been heard from for more'n two years. I wonder what happened to her. Seems to me I heard some tale about trouble aboard the Rover.'

'Yes, sir,' David said eagerly. 'My pa heard a story about some of her crew being picked up by another whaler. They'd been adrift three weeks in a whaleboat. One of 'em said there'd been a mutiny, sir, and he told about somebody being put ashore on a deserted island. They claimed they didn't know what had happened to Uncle Bob, but maybe he'd...'

'Don't get excited, son. You're not likely to be finding your Uncle Bob. But you still want to go whalin', do you?'

'Yes, sir.'

Again Captain Hunter looked him over. Then turned back to his maps.

David was afraid he was going to be refused, after all.

He had felt sure from Captain Hunter's interest in his uncle that he'd be given a chance and his hopes had run high. He stood there for what seemed hours, still twisting his cap, eyes fixed on the toes of his scuffed boots, not knowing whether he should say anything more or not.

'All right. I'll sign you on. Go get your gear and be back this afternoon. We sail at four.'

Captain Hunter gave a sign of dismissal.

'Thank you, sir.'

The boy turned on his heel and left the cabin, hardly daring to believe in his good luck.

'Here, there!'

It was Captain Hunter, and David hurried back.

'You've got to sign the papers, you know. You'll get a two hundred and fiftieth lay. Do you know what that means?'

'Yes, sir. When our oil's sold I get one two hundred and fiftieth of the profits of the voyage. I mean after I've paid for my outfit and anything I get from the slop chest while at sea.'

Captain Hunter grunted, and this time David left the cabin without being called back. He found Frank on deck waiting for him. The harpooner asked no questions. One look at the boy's face was enough to show that he had signed on.

'Run along and get your outfit,' he said. 'They'll fix you up at the Sign of the Whale. Tell 'em I sent you.'

Once again David found himself walking along the New Bedford street, but now he was no longer a farm boy; he was a seaman who had just signed up for his first voyage. At the Sign of the Whale he found himself a little embarrassed as to what a whaleman's outfit consisted of, but the fat, old proprietor, a former whaleman himself, needed no suggestions. As soon as the boy mentioned the Sea Turtle and Frank White, he began handing out a pile of equipment.

David was soon the proud possessor of a tarpaulin hat, heavy pantaloons and a bright red shirt, a thick Guernsey frock, and a pair of sea boots. These were for everyday wear. Then into the sea chest which he bought, he put the rest of his outfit: a heavy oilskin, two striped comforters, a monkey jacket, extra pants and shirts, warm underclothes, shoes, stockings, a bed quilt, a blanket, tin pot, tin pan, spoon, soap, needles, thread, and four jackknives.

It came to the huge sum of seventy-five dollars. David had never had so much money in the world. He hadn't it now. The outfitter would get it out of his future wages, and although the boy had a vague idea that he was being imposed upon, there didn't seem to be anything he could do about it. What did it matter, anyway? He borrowed a wheelbarrow to carry his new possessions and trundled it proudly down the waterfront.

When he reached the Sea Turtle, men were busy about her decks and a number of sailors were storing away some of the supplies and ship's gear. He was glad to see Frank. The friendly harpooner helped him get his chest aboard and down the steep ladder which led to the forecastle.

The air below decks was so thick that for a time he could make out nothing in the gloomy little compartment in the ship's bow which was to be his home for how many months, or even years, he didn't know. But as his eyes became accustomed to it, he saw that the forecastle was lined with bunks, two tiers of them, and that the little space remaining about the foremast, which cut right through the center of the room, was cluttered with sea chests. Nothing looked very clean and there was an acrid smell of smoke and perspiration.

David looked for an empty bunk. Some of them had already been appropriated. In two or three, men were lying asleep, snoring fearfully. As he stumbled about in the semi-darkness, he almost fell over one sailor stretched full length on the floor. The boy had heard of seamen being brought on board ship dead drunk.

Finally he found a place which no one seemed to have marked off, dragged his chest over to it, and threw some of his bedding on the hard boards. Then he clambered thankfully up the ladder and out into the cool, fresh air.

It was almost time to sail and David had no more than reached the deck when a man whom he took to be one of the officers, perhaps the first mate, began barking out a series of curt orders. They meant nothing to the boy. He had no idea of what to do. To keep out of the way of the sailors now rushing about the deck in the last-minute preparations for casting off, seemed his best policy.

No one paid any attention to him. It was clear that the officers relied wholly on the old hands and for the time being expected nothing from greenies like himself.

He could not afterwards have told how the Sea Turtle got under way. The scene to him was one of indescribable confusion. Ropes were cast off, ropes were pulled, ropes came slithering down on deck from somewhere aloft. No matter how fast David tried to dodge, he was always in danger of becoming entangled in a flying line. Whatever he did, he was in the way. The great sails began to flap in the breeze, to belly out as the wind caught them. Leaning against the rail and looking up at the straining canvas, he became so excited that he almost fell overboard.

It was just at this point that a sharp, unexpected kick reminded him that he was not a passenger aboard the Sea Turtle. He swung around to see the mate withdrawing his foot.

'Jump, you dunderhead!' the irate officer shouted at him. 'You're no good around here, but you ought to have enough sense to keep out of the way. Now make yourself useful. Here, grab this line and heave.'

David didn't know what the line was. He might have been hauling up the anchor or running up an ensign. But he didn't stop to resent the kick or the angry order. It was his first job on shipboard and he was determined to do it well. When the line would pull no longer, he hung on to it like grim death. He was afraid the mainsail might break away. He had horrible visions of the ship capsizing because he let go, and saw the Sea Turtle floating bottom up in an angry sea. It was with intense relief that he noticed Frank coming to his rescue. The harpooner slipped the line over its pin and made it fast with a few deft turns.

'So you've felt Mr. Starbuck's toe already,' Frank laughed. 'Never mind, you'll feel it again. He's a sharp one, Mr. Starbuck. Better go forward, lad, where he won't see you.'

The Sea Turtle was getting well under way and before long gained such an offing that the pilot, who had been directing her course out of the harbor, signaled the sailboat which had been accompanying them to draw up. As it ranged alongside he jumped from the whaler's bulwarks down onto its deck, and with a wave of his hand sped the Sea Turtle on her voyage. The vessel picked up after this farewell, and heading toward the open sea raced into the teeth of the wind. Her whole frame seemed to quiver as she plunged into the deep green seas rushing toward her, and the wind whistled merrily through her rigging.

Bracing himself against the forward rail, David felt a thrill of excitement such as he had never known before in his life. For the time being the mad plunges of the ship as she ploughed through the heavy seas kicked up by the rising wind, the pounding of waves against her sides, the increasing roll, did not bother him. Eagerly he looked back and forth from the slowly receding shore to the open sea which lay ahead. Daylight was fading, and with the loss of the sunlight which had given the December afternoon an unusual warmth, a bitter chill pervaded the air. The boy hugged himself close in his stout reefer.

Strange memories flitted quickly through his mind: Uncle Bob telling stories of his whaling voyages as they sat around the stove on just such a December night as this, his father warning him of the perils of the world as he set forth on his adventure, the bullying Portuguese sailor at the Crossed Harpoons with the livid scar on his cheek, Captain Hunter poring over his maps in his snug cabin. David threw back his head and stretched out his arms, welcoming the cold rush of wind on his face and the stinging salt spray. Unknown seas, unknown ports, unknown adventures lay ahead! He was going whaling!

III

FIRST DAYS AT SEA

Frank and David Coil Line

Chapter III

FIRST DAYS AT SEA

IF ANYONE who had noticed David that first night at
sea, joyously letting the spray dash over him as he
stood at the Sea Turtle's prow, could have seen him two
days later, he would not have known it was the same boy.
He lay huddled in his bunk, his blanket drawn up to his
chin, wishing he was anywhere in the world except aboard a
whaleship. For the Sea Turtle had run into heavy weather.
The little vessel pitched and rolled terribly, groaning in
every timber, and the miserable boy felt sure each time she
wallowed in the trough of the sea that she was going to sink.
He wished she would. He was so sick that nothing mattered
except his own misery.

The first day of bad weather he had tried to stay on deck.
The alarming way the vessel had of sliding down one wave
and then abruptly starting to climb the next, had given
him a queer sensation in the pit of his stomach, but he was
determined not to give in. But then his legs began to feel
wobbly, his head spun, and the impulse to lie down became
so strong he could not resist it. No one paid any attention
to him as he stumbled toward the hatchway and practically
fell down the steep ladder to the forecastle.

Once there he threw himself on his bunk. But it was no use. The smell of the burning lamp, of musty blankets, of bilge water, made him feel worse than he had felt on deck. Yet he couldn't get up. There was nothing to do but let go and be sick.

He had a queer dream that first night. He thought that he was back home on the farm, lying in bed, while in the next room his father and Uncle Bob talked of days at sea. Occasionally he could hear a part of the story his uncle was telling, then the low voice would die down. It was something about a quarrel. Someone in the crew had jumped on the third mate and thrown him to the deck.

'He was an ugly-looking Portuguese,' he seemed to hear his uncle say. 'They called him Dago something-or-other. If I hadn't caught him just in time, he'd have done for Charley just as sure as I'm sitting here. I saw the gleam of his knife. He was a mean customer, all right. I'll never forget him. Right across his cheek, from the corner of his eye almost to his mouth, he had a deep scar...'

David woke up suddenly. Dream or memory of something that had happened? He didn't know. And what was there about that story of the ugly Portuguese sailor with the scar on his face which seemed to have some connection with him? Then he remembered. The man at the Crossed Harpoons. They called him Dago Jack, and he had noticed the scar just before the fight had started. It must have been the same man. But everything was confused, as he lay there sick in his bunk. The forecastle seemed to revolve about him in dizzy circles while before his eyes danced a leering face with a livid scar.

When David finally recovered enough to get on deck again, he discovered that the Sea Turtle was far at sea, bowling along merrily with all canvas set. The fresh air made him feel a little better, and he even got his courage up to persuade the cook to give him something to eat. He staggered over to the windlass and sat down.

'A bit green about the gills, eh?'

David looked up and smiled feebly. It was Frank, looking so hale and hearty that the boy felt even worse.

'What do you think of goin' to sea now? I guess you wish you was back on the farm,' the harpooner said cheerfully. 'Never mind. We ain't struck any really stiff weather yet. You're pretty lucky. If we speak a homeward-bound ship, I suppose you'd want to be put aboard her.'

'No,' David answered stoutly. 'I'm all right now.'

He got up slowly, but had no more than taken a few steps to show that he now had his sea legs, than the ship gave a terrific roll. The world spun around before his eyes and he rushed to the rail.

Frank did not seem sympathetic.

'You've been sleeping too much. Now give me a hand here and it'll get your mind off yer troubles.'

The harpooner was going through the gear in one of the whaleboats and had David help him coil one of the long whalelines in its tub.

'You've got to get this just right,' he said. 'A single kink in the line's a sure ticket to Davy Jones's locker. I got caught once myself.'

'What happened?'

'Well, we were pullin' up on a big whale, just as quiet as a cat stalkin' a mouse. When we got close, I let my iron fly. It sank into his hump up to the hitches and that there whale lit out like a colt stung by a wasp. The line started to run. I was just about to throw my second harpoon when darned if a loose kink didn't catch my arm. Before I knew what had happened... Hey, there, watch what you're doin'!'

Frank grunted and leaned down to straighten out the line they were coiling.

'Yes, yes,' David said impatiently. He had forgotten his seasickness.

'What was I sayin'?' Frank glanced keenly at the boy whose face was beginning to get back some of its natural color. 'Oh, yes. Well, I went over the side of that boat clean as a whistle. Yes, sir, I thought I was a goner. I was bein' pulled through the water so fast it nearly skinned off my eyebrows.'

Again Frank seemed to forget his story.

'How'd you get loose?'

'I cut the line.'

'You cut the line?'

'Sure. After a minute I thought to myself, "This is no way to catch a whale, Frank, my boy. You're goin' to drown if you don't watch out." So I felt around for my knife, and when I got holt of it I cut the line.'

'Then did they pick you up?'

'Well, I wouldn't be here if they hadn't. They dragged me aboard and poured the water out of me. But I sure was sorry we missed that whale. He was a good one. Feelin' any better?'

David grinned sheepishly.

'Sure, I feel fine.'

Frank's treatment had really worked, and with something else to think about David began to get over his feeling that he was about to be sick any moment. It was a fortunate thing. The ship's officers had made no attempt to get any work out of the green hands these first few days, but now they were ready to start whipping them into shape. That very afternoon the whole crew was summoned on deck to be divided into watches and boat crews. Captain Hunter came up to give them the talk which every whaling captain made after his vessel was well at sea.

'Well, I suppose you all know why you're here,' he started, pacing back and forth on the quarterdeck and looking down at the men gathered in the ship's waist. 'You're out to make a whalin' voyage. What we want's oil. That's what we're after, you understand? But we got to work to get it. When you're ordered to do somethin', you'll do it. Otherwise I'll know the reason why.

'There'll be no loafin' aboard the Sea Turtle; there'll be no refusin' duty. If any of you have anything to complain about, come aft and see me. I ain't plannin' to drive you; I'll treat you square. But no funny business, either.

'You'll get good grub and plenty of it. The "doctor" will take care of that. We'll treat you well. But no fightin' aboard this ship. No drinkin' and no card playin'. And there won't be any swearin' either. Any trouble forrard and there'll be more trouble aft. We're goin' to have strict discipline. I'm givin' you plenty of warning now. All right. The mates will take you in hand now and teach you what you ought to know.'

Captain Hunter glared down at the crew, turned on his heel, and went back to his cabin.

A tall, dark man who had stood off to one side while Captain Hunter was talking now stepped forward. David noticed that it was the officer who had given him that unexpected kick on his first night at sea.

'You in the dark shirt there,' he ordered, pointing at one

of the crew, 'step over to the port rail. All right, Mr. Macy.'

David had not seen this other officer, who turned out to be the second mate. He was a short, fair-haired man, the exact opposite of the first mate, whose name the boy now remembered was Mr. Starbuck. Whereas the latter seemed to wear a perpetual scowl, Mr. Macy appeared to be enjoying some secret joke, about to break out into laughter any moment. As the two of them proceeded to choose the men for their watches, David hoped fervently Mr. Macy would pick him out.

The process took some time. In addition to her captain and two mates; the harpooners; the 'doctor,' as the ship's cook was called; a steward, a carpenter, a cooper, and a blacksmith, the Sea Turtle had eighteen men before the mast. She could man four whaleboats. The old hands were chosen carefully by the two officers. When only the new men were left, neither Mr. Starbuck nor Mr. Macy seemed to care which ones were in his watch. David found himself in that of Mr. Starbuck.

What he now hoped was that he would be assigned to a boat crew. He realized that he was so young that it would not be likely. Some of the foremast hands would have to be left aboard as shipkeepers whenever they lowered after whales.

'Ever been to sea before?'

Mr. Starbuck was standing in front of him, looking him over carefully with that harsh scowl.

'No, sir, but...'

'No "buts" when you're talking to me. Understand? It's "yes, sir" or "no, sir." I don't suppose you ever pulled an oar in your life.'

'No, sir.'

'You look pretty strong. You've got long arms. Do you think you could keep up on a four-mile pull? Do you think you'd lose your nerve if the whale turned on the boat and flipped his flukes in your direction?'

'Yes, sir. I mean, no, sir.'

'Yes, sir! No, sir! Speak up. Haven't you got a tongue in your head?'

Mr. Starbuck was suddenly furious. He seemed to swell up and his face became a deep crimson. He turned savagely on the startled boy.

'No more of your lip! Didn't I tell you not to "but" me? When I ask a question I want a civil answer, and I intend to have one. Anything more from you and I'll have to teach you some sea manners. Now, then. If you want to pull an oar, you'll have to prove you can do it.'

With this he turned away and called to a seaman on the other side of the ship, a man whom David had not seen during those days he had felt so seasick.

'Here, there,' Mr. Starbuck shouted. 'I've picked out a crew for the starboard boat. You're her harpooner. Try to teach these landlubbers what they're supposed to know.'

As the seaman thus summoned made his way across the deck, David recognized him with a sinking feeling. It was Dago Jack.

The Portuguese, whose quarters in the steerage with the other harpooners gave him no occasion to visit the forecastle, was no less surprised to see David. The angry flush which spread over his face showed that he remembered the boy well and had not forgotten his interference when he was teasing the cat at the Crossed Harpoons.

'So you've shipped aboard the Sea Turtle,' he said in a sneering tone. 'Ain't that nice!'

David made no answer.

'Listen to this. If you ever get in my way again, if you ever try to interfere in anythin' I want to do, you won't get off as easy as you did the other night.'

Looking about carefully and lowering his voice to a menacing whisper, he went on:

'Do you understand? There won't be any chance for your friend Frank to help you either. Anyone who gets in Dago Jack's way is good and sorry. You wouldn't be the first.'

With this Dago Jack walked off, thrusting out his thick underlip. David did not know whether he really saw or imagined that the Portuguese moved his hand toward the knife stuck in his belt. But he remembered his uncle's story. He was sure now that he had really overheard it, not dreamed it, and he was sure Dago Jack was the same man.

IV

OLD TIM'S STORIES

How About a Piece of Steak?

Chapter IV

WITH the division of the crew into watches, life aboard the Sea Turtle began to take on a regular routine. The ship's course lay on a generally south-easterly route across the Atlantic and apparently Captain Hunter planned to stop at the Azores, where the whalers often called to pick up supplies and perhaps recruit a few more men for their crews. Good weather made the passage an easy and pleasant one. Little occurred to break the monotony of the long days at sea.

David gradually became accustomed to his new life. The two mates lost no time in teaching the green hands how to set and trim the sails, how to take their tricks at the wheel, how to stand watch at the masthead. The supplies were also broken out, overhauled carefully and stored away again. The rigging was gone over, the whaleboats conditioned and made ready for lowering, the harpoons and lances sharpened. There was plenty for all hands to do on these first few weeks of the voyage, and the mates had them working every minute of their watch on deck.

His first trip aloft was an experience which David never forgot. He was busily scrubbing the deck one morning

when Mr. Starbuck shouted an order from the quarterdeck:
'Tumble up aloft, and lay out on the yards.'

Several of the crew quickly sprang into the rigging and
began to climb rapidly. David hesitated, glancing fearfully
up at the swaying mast. But he knew it had to be done some
day, and getting a firm grip on the shrouds he started on
what to him seemed a perilous journey.

'Get along there,' he heard the mate call. 'Hey, Dago
Jack. Teach those green hands what to do when I order
'em aloft.'

Looking down over his shoulder the boy saw Dago Jack
with a wicked grin jump into the rigging below him. He
held a short piece of tarred line in his hand. A moment later
David felt the sharp sting of the rope's end across the back
of his legs.

'Up with you, up with you!' the Portuguese shouted.
'How does that feel? I'll learn you to get aloft. Jump, you
chicken-hearted son of a sea-cook!'

David felt hot with resentment, but he knew there was
nothing he could do. Dago Jack was only following out
Mr. Starbuck's orders, and to be taught their ropes with a
rope's end was a common experience for green hands.
Gritting his teeth, he determined not to let Dago Jack have
any more fun at his expense. Without looking either up or
down, he climbed up the rigging, reached his yard, and,
clinging to anything he could get his hands on, blindly followed the man ahead of him.

The wind had freshened. That was why the men had
been sent aloft to take in sail. The Sea Turtle was pitching
and rolling badly, and from where he was the deck appeared
to David to be miles below him. If he lost his grip! But
David did not dare to think of that. The swinging mast, the

flapping sail, the horizon sweeping up and down in terrifying dips and rises, set him trembling all over.

Somehow he managed to do his part in getting in sail. Every moment he thought would be his last. The canvas billowed out, the lines cut into his hands, his feet were always on the point of slipping. Only the thought of Dago Jack and his rope's end kept him from funking.

When a little later he was back again on the stable planks of the deck, he did not believe he could ever again have the courage to climb up the rigging. But the next time proved to be much easier. On his third trip aloft, he began to feel like a veteran. Before he knew it, he enjoyed nothing so much as a quick climb to the masthead. He became as much at home in the shrouds as he had been in the branches of the old apple tree where he used to hide from his sister as a small boy.

David also began to make friends. Neither Captain Hunter nor Mr. Starbuck ever appeared to notice him, except to give an order, but Mr. Macy had a kind word now and then. There was Frank, of course, but he was in a different watch. David had long talks with Old Tim the blacksmith. It was from him that he began to learn something about whales and whaling as the Sea Turtle sailed leisurely toward the Azores.

One day the blacksmith set David to work turning his grindstone while he sharpened the harpoons and lances. The weather was calm and far warmer than it had been so far on the voyage.

'Tim,' the boy asked after he had worked some time, 'is a whale really the biggest fish in the ocean?'

The blacksmith looked up and stood for a moment rubbing the heavy stubble on the side of his chin with a meditative hand.

'Fish, your grandmother,' he said at last. 'A whale ain't a fish. That's what comes of growin' up on a farm. You're just plain ignorant.'

Tim shook his head sadly.

'A whale's an animal. It's got to breathe just like you and me. It swims like a fish, sure, but it's got to come up and spout and get some air or it would drown. Yep, a whale's an animal, and more'n that, it's what they call a mammal. It feeds its young milk. Don't you ever go callin' a whale a fish again.'

As Tim turned back to his work, David started to ask him another question. But there was no need. The blacksmith liked nothing better than to talk about whales whenever he found anyone who would listen to him.

'Yes, sir, a whale's an animal. It's the biggest one there is. There ain't nothin' can size up to a whale on land or sea. We measure 'em by the barrels of oil they give. Now a good, big whale may try-out sixty barrels and he'd be about sixty feet long. It'd be seven feet the width of his flukes — that's his tail, you know — and he might have a jaw fourteen feet long. And that blubber overcoat he wears, that stuff we get the oil out of, would be anywhere from five to nine inches thick. Ever heard of Japan?'

'Yes,' said David doubtfully.

'Well, they say those Japanners cut up a whale into steaks. A big whale will feed a hundred and twenty thousand of 'em!'

'Are all whales alike?' the boy asked.

'No, there's lots of different kinds of whales. There're sperm whales. You can tell them because they've only one spout. And there're right whales. They've two spouts. Those are the only two worth a dern, and those are the ones we're after, specially spermaceti. They may be ugly, those big bull sperms, but they've got lots of oil. I remember one time...'

The blacksmith stopped to light his pipe. He was warming to his subject. Neither he nor David was doing much work.

'Yes,' said the boy eagerly, 'you remember...'

'Now wait a minute. Not so fast. About these here whales. Do you know what they eat?'

'No.'

'Well, it's a funny thing. The right whale's got a great big head and a mouth you could drive a wagon into. What he eats is some stuff called brit. It's little tiny animals that float on the top of the water. They're yellow. I've seen the ocean so covered with 'em that you'd think it was a field of wheat. So when the right whale wants to eat, he just opens his mouth and swims along the surface. In goes the brit. But a lot of water goes in too.

'Now the right whale's got a linin' to his mouth made of slabs of baleen, what we call whalebone, which is sort of like a sieve. So what does he do? He closes down these slabs and pushes the water out of his mouth. The brit gets caught on the edges. Then he can swallow his dinner without gettin' swamped.

'The sperm whale's a different story. He's got a jaw like a... like a... well, like a sperm whale. It's full of teeth, sharp ones, too. So he don't eat brit. He eats squid and he just...'

'What do you mean, squid?'

'Why a squid's a giant octopus. He's a fierce-lookin' crittur with long writhing arms. But those arms don't bother a sperm whale any. He lies in wait for the squid

with his jaw hangin' open like a trapdoor. When the squid
swims in to look things over — bang, the trapdoor closes.
He's chewed up in no time at all. Then the sperm whale
opens up his jaw and waits for another squid. I ain't never
seen it myself, but... why, what's worryin' you?'

'I dunno,' David answered. 'I just wondered. Say,
Tim, could a whale really have swallowed Jonah?'

The blacksmith shook his head slowly.

'I don't just see how he could. That is, and Jonah live
to tell the story. A whale's big enough all right. I heard of
a sailor once that fell into a whale's mouth and the whale
choked or something and coughed him up. But you see if it
was a right whale tried to swallow Jonah, he'd have got
caught in the baleen. If it was a sperm whale, he'd have
been chewed up. No, I don't reckon that whale really
swallowed Jonah.'

Tim picked up a harpoon, felt its edge reflectively.

'Has a whale got eyes and ears?' David asked.

'That's another funny thing,' answered the blacksmith,
only too glad to go on. 'A whale's got eyes all right, though
they're so small you'd never notice 'em, and I guess it's
got ears, though I never seen 'em at all. Anyway, it catches
on to danger mighty quick somehow or other.

'I've seen a whole school of whales, feeding quiet as you
please, and all of a sudden they rush off just as if one of 'em
had seen the boat and given all the others warnin'. Maybe
they was playin' about in the water like a lot of kittens,
bobbin' up and down in the waves and slappin' the water
with their flukes so loud you could hear 'em aboard ship;
then the next thing you know, they've all sounded and
that's the last of 'em.

'Another time I remember we harpooned a whale. Way

off in the distance was a lot of others. Instead of soundin', they all swam over to the harpooned whale just as if he'd told 'em he was in trouble. They're peculiar critturs. They don't make any noise. I mean they don't call to each other. But somehow they seem to let one another know what's goin' on.'

'When they sound, do they go down deep?'

'They sure do. I guess to the bottom of the ocean. One time we was in a boat and the whale we was fast to sounded. We let out the whole line. It weren't enough. Then we bent another line on to that one. The whale was still goin' down. Why, we gave him almost a mile of line and then had to cut it. You lose a lot of whales that way.'

For a time Tim went on with his work and David turned the grindstone while he sharpened the edges on some of his harpoons. The boy had a lot to think about. He hadn't known much about whales before and had no idea of their peculiarities. He wondered how soon he would see one. Looking up, he scanned the horizon closely. But there was no sign of any telltale spout. Sea and sky blended imperceptibly in the distance. Tim had spoken of big, ugly bulls; he'd heard of fighting whales from Uncle Bob.

'What was that story you were going to tell, Tim?'

'Are we sharpenin' harpoons or are we talkin' about whales?'

The blacksmith sounded abrupt and David looked up in surprise. But it was only a gesture in support of discipline. Another moment and Tim was again in full flight.

'It was a calm day,' he started, 'and when we lowered there was hardly a breath stirrin'. But what a chase the whale we was after gave us! We'd just about pull up on him, and he'd sound. There we'd be not knowin' where he was goin' to come up next, and then somebody would sight his spout about a mile off.

'"She blows! She blows!" the mate would holler, and we'd be off again.

'Well, this lasted about two hours and then we fooled the crittur. He was always headin' a little northeast, so next time he sounded, we headed that way ourselves and waited. Suddenly there was a tremendous commotion. The sea began to heave like it was a cyclone had hit us. And before we knew what had happened, there was the whale so close to the boat we could almost reach out and touch him. The spray shootin' out of his spout-hole drenched every man of us.

'"Let him have it!" sings out the mate dancin' up and down in the stern of the boat. "Let him have it!"

'I was harpooner and I let him have it, all right. I heaved the iron so hard and fast that whale never knew what hit him. He gave a sort of jump which took him almost clear off the water, and then, by cripes, he gave a sidesweep with his flukes that struck us amidships.

'It all happened so sudden-like that the next thing we knew every man-jack of us was swimmin' for dear life. The boat was smashed to pulp. I grabbed an oar, but I didn't know how long I could hang on. I was afraid that whale would come for us again. When they get fightin' mad, you don't know what they'll do. So I looks around with my heart just about jumpin' out of my mouth. There was the whale, wallowin' in the swells, and not makin' a move.

'"That's a funny thing," I thought to myself. "You'd think he'd either make for us or sound." So I watched him for a while. Then it dawned on me. He was dead. Yes, sir, he was dead as a doornail. No doubt of it. I'd sunk that harpoon so deep into him that it had done for him right then and there.

'That took a load off my mind, all right, but what were we goin' to do next? Our boat was smashed to splinters. The dern whale had led us such a chase that the ship wasn't anywhere in sight. There we were, six of us adrift in mid-ocean, hangin' on to oars and spars and bits of wreckage.'

Tim paused for a moment while David waited impatiently for him to go on. Here was adventure. This was the sort of thing he had come whaling for. But what was the end of the story?

'There that whale lay,' the blacksmith said at last, 'rollin' in the swells like a mountain of blubber, and he looked pretty good to us. He was more solid than a broken plank. I was the first to push over to him and when I was alongside I got a grip on his hump and heaved myself up on his back. He rolled a bit and it was wet and slippery, but settin' on a whale is a lot better than settin' on nothin' at all.

'In a few minutes all six of us was perched there, happy as you please.

'After a while we began to get hungry. We'd been out in the boat all day without a bite since breakfast and salt air gives you a hearty appetite.

'"How about a piece of steak?" I asks the mate.

'"Sure, and I'd like some plum duff, too," he answers.

'"I ain't got the plum duff with me," I said, "but if you don't mind your meat a little raw..."

'With that I whips out my sheath knife and starts slicin' a piece of blubber off the whale's hump...'

'What sort of a fish story is this?' boomed a cheerful voice just as Tim began smacking his lips over an imaginary slice of whale steak. 'Fillin' the boy up with a lot of sea yarns, eh?'

Frank lounged over to where the blacksmith was working and sat down on a coil of rope. He had brought two harpoons to get them sharpened.

'Go on, Tim; go on. I know it's a pack of lies. But so's every whalin' yarn you hear aboard this ship.'

'Pack of lies! Why, this story's nothin' to some I could tell. Why, one time off the coast of Chile...'

'Get along with you, get along with you,' Frank interrupted. 'What happened to you, settin' there on the back of your whale cuttin' steaks off his hump. That's a good one! Finish your yarn. I want to see if you can put a better edge on these irons than you did last time.'

Tim did not seem any too pleased with an addition to his audience, but he went on:

'Yes, sir, we cut ourselves some steaks off that whale and we ate 'em. They was a little raw and blubbery, but we was hungry. Then we began to worry about whether the ship was goin' to pick us up. It was comin' on night and the wind was risin'. The whale was rollin' so much we could hardly hang on. One fellow who let go his grip on the crittur's hump started to slide down his back as if it was a greased chute. But he grabbed my leg and pulled himself back.

'I tell you, it was gettin' dern serious. You can't stay on a whale's back all night in a rough sea. We didn't know what was goin' to happen. Then suddenly one of the men raised a shout:

'"There's a boat! there's a boat!" he sang out.

'We set up such a hollerin' and yellin' as ever's been heard on the Pacific Ocean. If the men in that boat heard us, we were saved. If they didn't, we wouldn't have a chance. I guess I said it was gettin' dark. Anyway, we could only see the boat dimly. It seemed to stop. Then it started up again — pullin' away from us.

'We yelled our lungs out. We just about burst 'em. That shout could have been heard two miles. Then we stopped to listen. There was a faint answerin' cry. The boat was turned around and it was comin' our direction.

'When they got close to us, we just slipped off the whale into the water. They had to haul us aboard. But did it feel good to be in a boat again!'

Tim had let his pipe go out and now stopped to light it.

'That's a grand yarn,' broke in Frank, 'but see if you can put an edge on this harpoon which'll help us to get some real whale steaks. Grind away there, David. I'm pretty particular about my irons.'

The blacksmith put down his pipe and taking Frank's harpoon began to work over it carefully.

'Did you ever kill a whale with a harpoon?' he asked, without looking up.

'Never did,' answered the harpooner. 'Never had an iron that would do that trick. I've seen 'em killed with one blow of the lance, but never with a harpoon.'

Tim grunted.

'Well, I'll put an edge on this one such as you never felt before. It won't be my fault if you miss your next whale.'

'It won't, won't it?' said Frank good-naturedly. 'I dunno about that.'

All this time David was turning the heavy grindstone. Tim couldn't seem to get satisfied with the edge he was putting on the harpoon. First he'd hold one side of its triangular-shaped head to the stone, then another. The boy thought he never would be through.

'Here you are, Frank,' he said at last. 'If this don't suit you, I'll eat my...'

He paused for a moment, rubbing his hand over his chin.

'Holy mackerel! I guess I must have fergot to shave this mornin'.'

He took the head of the harpoon in his hand and began to scrape his cheek with the iron's razor-like edge.

Frank let out a bellow of joy.

'By the great horn spoon!' he shouted in his thundering voice. 'Tim's shavin' himself with a harpoon!'

The watch on deck quickly gathered around and watched in admiring awe as the blacksmith scraped away at his bristly chin as if a harpoon shave were the most natural thing in the world. David stood by with mouth open.

'At least I turned the grindstone,' he thought to himself.

V
DAVID PULLS A BONER

The Look-Out

Chapter V

DAVID PULLS A BONER

IT WAS not many days after this conversation about whales that an incident occurred which David thought for a time would spoil his whole whaling voyage.

So far not a single whale had been sighted. Lookouts were always kept at the mastheads, for many whales were taken in the vicinity of the Azores. There was no telling how soon the Sea Turtle might run upon a school or at least some lone bull which might have wandered off on his own. But none was seen.

Once or twice the boats were lowered for practice pulls. David had hoped to be included in the crew of the starboard boat, but when Mr. Starbuck ordered Dago Jack to get ready to lower, the Portuguese casually ignored him. David was sure it was just spite. The bow oar was a clumsy, awkward man who very evidently had never been in a boat before. The boy knew he could make a better job of it. He leaned over the rail bitterly disappointed, as the boat shoved off, and Mr. Starbuck, with angry curses, tried to get his crew to pull together.

One afternoon when the boats returned from a practice pull, Captain Hunter called all hands on deck. When the watch below had turned out and the entire crew, except for the lookouts and steersman, were gathered in the waist, he stalked down from the quarterdeck. Then with great solemnity he nailed a silver dollar to the mainmast.

'First man to raise a whale,' he barked, 'gets the dollar.'

After this announcement not only the lookouts but most of the watch on deck kept an eager eye out for possible sight of a whale. A dollar was a dollar. Even aboard ship. It meant a good deal of tobacco from the ship's slop chest and there were few of the foremast hands who weren't either smoking or chewing constantly. David did not want tobacco. There wasn't anything he needed from the slop chest. But he wouldn't have minded having that dollar just the same.

He was thinking about it the next time he found himself on lookout, hoping against hope that he would be lucky enough to raise the first whale. Then perhaps Mr. Starbuck would give him a chance to pull the bow oar in his boat despite Dago Jack.

It was a warm, lazy afternoon. The Sea Turtle was sailing slowly with a following wind, her sails spread to catch every breath of the gentle breeze. She sank and rose again, sank and rose again. Perched securely in the crosstrees, the boy was lulled by the gentle motion. The sun beat down. The water shimmered beneath the burning glare. He tried to keep alert, his eyes searching the horizon, but it was all he could do not to fall asleep. His thoughts drifted off idly.

He wished that he was back home on the farm. What would he be doing on such an afternoon as this? It was like a day of early spring, too early for ploughing. He might have been able to wander off by himself, down by the brook where he used to fish. It would be pleasant to lie on his back and look up at the clouds floating overhead.

He remembered one time when his father had sent him off to drive home a cow which had broken through the pasture fence. He had found her quietly feeding in the meadow through which the brook ran. Instead of starting at once to drive her home, he had lain down just for a minute. He didn't know how it had happened, but when he got up, it was beginning to get dark. The cow was nowhere in sight.

'I guess I must have fallen asleep,' David said to himself.

At the sound of his own voice, he started up. Where was he now? Was he still hunting for that cow? But as he looked about it was not a green pasture which he saw; he was surrounded on all sides by the limitless blue of sea and sky. He was aboard the Sea Turtle. He was looking for whales, not for cows.

Suddenly he gave a start which almost tumbled him off his high perch.

There was something white, far ahead, off the port bow. He looked again. It was caught in the sunlight. Could it be a whale's spout? There it was again! It must be a whale!

He knew what he should do. He knew the whaleman's call.

'There she blows! There she blows!' he cried out at the top of his voice. 'She blows! She blo——ws!'

He was sure of it now. He saw any number of spouts. There must be a whole school of whales. He could see their glistening backs reflecting the bright glare of the sun. The silver dollar danced before his eyes. Wild with excitement, he repeated the long-drawn-out call.

'There she blows! Off the port bow! She blows! She blo——ws!'

In an instant the ship awoke from its mid-afternoon calm.
The men on deck sprang to their feet and jumped into the
rigging to catch for themselves a sight of the first whale.
Up the forecastle hatchway rushed several hands from the
watch below. The harpooners hurried to their boats to see
if everything was in shape for lowering. Mr. Starbuck was
giving the order to stand by just as Captain Hunter emerged
from the cabin companionway. The Sea Turtle was ready
for action.

'Where away? Where away?' came the call from the
quarterdeck.

For a moment there was no answering shout. Then from
the lookout on the foremast came the unexpected reply:

'School of porpoises off the port bow, sir.'

It was true. That flash of white David had glimpsed in
the distance had not been a filmy jet of vapor from a whale's
spout. Those dark objects reflecting the sun so brightly
were not whales. They were porpoises.

When no other voice had taken up his cry of 'There she
blows!' the boy had had a sinking feeling. He had not
dared answer Captain Hunter's call. His mistake was now
all too clear. He wished the earth would open up and
swallow him; he wished the Sea Turtle would sink quietly
and quickly to the depths of the sea.

Captain Hunter without a word went back to his cabin.
But Mr. Starbuck had something to say.

'Who gave that call?' he shouted fiercely, stamping about
the quarterdeck. 'Who's the dunderhead that don't know
a whale from a porpoise? Come down out of there, you
blithering idiot! I got something to say to you. I'll teach
you to know a porpoise from a whale. I'll teach you to
play a joke like that. Shake a leg there!'

David scrambled down and fearfully approached the quarterdeck.

For a full minute Mr. Starbuck eyed him with disgust. It was clear the boy had not been playing a practical joke. It was clear he had really thought he had sighted a whale. He stood there so thoroughly discomfited, so completely crestfallen, that it was pitiful. But sympathy was not Mr. Starbuck's strong point.

'So you're the fine sailor who don't know a porpoise from a whale!' he said caustically. 'What are your eyes for, anyway? I don't know what to do with you. Bread and water in the ship's run is what you really deserve. But I'll give you one more chance. No shore leave when we call at Fayal, though.'

Mr. Starbuck started to walk off and then turned back.

'In the meantime, report to the galley. You're under the cook's orders until you hear from me again. We'll see if peeling onions for a while ain't good for your eyes.'

The 'doctor' aboard the Sea Turtle was a burly negro called Sam, so fat that he could hardly squeeze through his galley door. He was not ill-natured, but he was lazy. Unexpectedly given an assistant, under his own orders, he wanted to get all the work out of him he could. David was doomed to spend hour after hour in the stuffy galley, cooking up the crew's rations of salt junk or dried vegetables, while Sam lazily watched him from an improvised seat made out of a wooden crate. The boy got so sick of the sight of food that he could hardly eat.

But the climax of this unfortunate experience came when they finally reached the Azores and the Sea Turtle lay at anchor in the harbor of Fayal.

David had rushed out on deck at the first cry of 'Land

ho!' and stood there watching the shore line gradually draw near with impatient longing. He would have given a good deal to be able to get his feet on firm ground again. He couldn't believe that Mr. Starbuck was really going to refuse him shore leave. The glistening white walls of Fayal's buildings, the church towers, the steep slopes of the hill behind the town, all made him eager to get ashore if only for an hour or two.

'Look pretty good, eh?'

David turned around angrily. He knew that sneering voice. He never seemed able to get away from it. Whenever anything went wrong, Dago Jack was at hand to rub it in. He wasn't afraid of the Portuguese. Some day he'd have it out with him, knife or no knife. If it came to a fight, he thought there would be enough of the crew on his side to assure fair play. Except for one special crony, a furtive, ill-natured seaman with a whining voice and shifty eyes, called 'Spider,' Dago Jack didn't have many friends. He kept very much to himself.

'It looks good,' the Portuguese continued, 'and it's even better when you get ashore. But I guess you're too busy in the galley...'

David would have liked to swing on his tormentor when Mr. Starbuck intervened.

'Get back there in the galley,' he ordered.

The boy turned around and walked off slowly, feeling very sorry for himself. What did he come whaling for, anyway? At that moment he was sure that he would spend the rest of the voyage in the galley—peeling onions. He would never get a chance to go ashore, never get a chance to lower after whales.

Everyone else in the crew had an opportunity to visit

Fayal in the next few days. David saw the boat crews starting off eagerly, and late at night heard them coming back boisterously. Tall tales were told in the forecastle of their shore adventures, and the boy would lie in his bunk pretending to sleep while his companions described what they had seen and the grog shops they had visited.

Water was taken aboard and a quantity of fresh supplies — fruits and vegetables. Two Portuguese were added to the crew. But more interesting for David, in fact the only interesting thing which served to break the monotony of his enforced stay on shipboard, was when Sam came proudly back from his afternoon of liberty with a little black monkey. The boy promptly appropriated it as his special pet.

Its wizened face wore a mournful expression which well suited David's mood, but it was such a lively animal that he decided to call it Hoppo. The two became close friends. The monkey followed him about whatever he was doing and slept at the foot of his bunk.

'The next time I'm sent aloft,' David thought to himself, 'I'll take Hoppo with me and perhaps he'll keep me awake.' He even imagined that he might teach the monkey to keep a lookout.

VI

THE STORM

Mr. Starbuck's Hat

Chapter VI

THE STORM

AFTER leaving Fayal the Sea Turtle cruised for a few days on the whaling grounds which lie off the Azores, but without any luck. Then Captain Hunter turned his vessel's bow to the southwest and started on the long leg of the outward voyage to the Brazil Banks and Cape Horn. There was little chance of raising whales. Day followed day, week followed week, with monotonous regularity. It was one aspect of a whaling voyage on which David had never counted.

Everything always seemed to be the same. The sky was always a clear blue, the sea a deeper blue, and the white sails of the Sea Turtle were the only thing in all that vast expanse of sea and sky which seemed to have a life of their own. The boy often looked up at them wonderingly as they stretched out taut so far above his head, and for a moment the sheer beauty of the billowing canvas would strangely stir him.

He wanted to race up the shrouds with Hoppo on his back, climb out on a yard or make his way to the cross-trees. He wanted to get as far from the galley as he possibly could and let the fresh South Atlantic breezes blow away the smell of stale food which seemed to hang about him like an invisible cloak. But he did not dare. Ordered to the galley, he was afraid Mr. Starbuck would find him out. To run afoul of the first mate for any further infraction of ship's discipline might bring all sorts of wrath down upon his head.

Frank tried to console him.

'What's the matter, David?' he asked when he discovered the boy leaning against the rail one afternoon with a face so long and woebegone that he looked as if he had just had the saddest possible news from home. 'What's the matter?'

'How long am I going to have to work in this dodgasted galley?' was the boy's answering question. 'All I do is peel potatoes, and peel onions, scrub pots and pans. It's all I do the livelong day. Is it going to last all voyage? Aren't I ever going to get a chance to be a real whaleman?'

The harpooner laughed.

'Don't get het up, lad. Why, this voyage's hardly started. There ain't ever much doin' on the South Atlantic run. Let's see. We've been gone a couple of months, ain't we? Well, it'll be a couple more, maybe three or four more, before we get around the Horn and up to the Pacific grounds.'

'That don't help,' the boy said discouragedly. 'When we do get there, I'll still be working in the galley. I don't believe Mr. Starbuck will ever let me lower after a whale.'

'Wait and see, wait and see,' Frank declared in a tone of conviction. 'There'll be plenty of work for all hands then. Don't think they'll keep a husky lad like you helpin' out Sam all the time. He can get along without you, and the time'll come when they need you in a boat. Maybe not the first time we lower, but soon enough. You'll get your chance — unless you still think every porpoise is a whale.'

Frank was called away and, as he turned back toward the galley, David tried to feel encouraged. If he could only somehow get into Mr. Starbuck's good graces! He was sitting staring at the blackened ceiling, a curled onion peel dangling from his knife, when a sound of scuffling and shouting broke out on deck.

'What the merry blazes! Confound that bloomin' monkey! Spring, you dunderhead. Catch him, I say; catch him!'

David popped out of the galley to witness an exciting scene which he would have enjoyed even more hugely if only he had dared to laugh.

Mr. Starbuck was rushing madly across the deck in full pursuit of Hoppo, and the agile little monkey held firmly grasped in one paw the irate mate's hat. How he had succeeded in snatching it off Mr. Starbuck's head, the boy could only guess, but, with the prize in his grasp, the monkey showed no intention of dropping it and nimbly dodged the mate's frantic efforts to catch him. Mr. Starbuck, very red in the face, was cursing furiously and calling on all hands to help him. Curiously enough, the efforts of the men on deck seemed only to result in more confusion. There was a great rushing to and fro, but whenever one of the sailors seemed about to get his hands on the monkey, someone else would unaccountably bump into him and little Hoppo would escape through their tangled legs.

There was no doubt the monkey was enjoying the chase. For some time he dodged about the deck, now scrambling up on one of the boats, now jumping into the rigging, and now retracing his flight to regain the quarterdeck where he would sit on the rail. Always he held the mate's hat clutched in his paw.

'Hold on!' Mr. Starbuck cried at last. 'Where's Sam?

Now, then, you good-for-nothing sea cook, catch that goldarned monkey of yours or I'll lambast the hide off you.'

Sam lumbered into the galley and came out with an
orange which he held out invitingly toward Hoppo. The
monkey looked at it quizzically; then looked at the hat in
his paw. He seemed to realize that an exchange was offered,
but he didn't want to accept it. As the cook drew near, he
leaped to the deck and scampered off.

Mr. Starbuck made another lunge at him and several of
the crew started off in shouting pursuit. Again they unaccountably failed to catch him, although one man once
actually had his hands on the animal. Then with a backward glance over his shoulder, Hoppo jumped into the rigging
and quickly climbed the shrouds to the topmast yardarm.
There he sat chattering excitedly, the hat still in his paw.

The entire crew were now on deck and appeared ready to
rush aloft *en masse* in pursuit of the monkey. But Mr.
Starbuck was afraid Hoppo would drop his precious hat
overboard.

'Stay where you are!' he shouted. 'Stop your confounded
yellin' at the monkey. Do you want him to drop the hat?
You, there' — and he pointed at David — 'climb up and
catch him. I've seen him playin' around with you. If you
can't get him now, I'll know the reason why.'

The boy started off, wondering how he was going to get
hold of Hoppo without making him drop the hat. Everyone
watched him as he climbed up the rigging and then gingerly
began to crawl out on the yard, speaking softly to Hoppo.
Slowly he drew close to the monkey; put out his hand.
But the moment the boy touched him, the monkey squeezed
still farther out on the yard beyond his reach. David
edged along a little more and again reached out. This time

Hoppo could move no farther; he was cornered. Seeing that the game was up, he jumped over on the boy's shoulder, but as he did so he flung the hat with a broad sweep of his arm well over the side of the ship. Another moment and it was floating in the Sea Turtle's wake.

'Lower the starboard...' began Mr. Starbuck, and then stopped. Captain Hunter had come on deck, and, catching sight of the broad grin on his usually stern-looking face, the mate thought better of his command. Scowling fiercely, he turned around and took his ruffled dignity to the cabin.

David climbed down the rigging with Hoppo still on his shoulder. A little later the monkey might have been seen, and it was perhaps fortunate Mr. Starbuck had not come on deck, sitting on the rail sucking an orange. Someone had given it to him even though the mate's fine hat was lost forever.

How Mr. Starbuck had looked when Hoppo snatched the hat off his head, how Frank had tripped up another of the harpooners just as he seemed about to catch the monkey, and how Captain Hunter had stood there grinning, formed a topic of endless conversation in the forecastle. It was about the only thing out of the ordinary that happened during the whole time between leaving Fayal and reaching that point off the South American coast where rounding Cape Horn began to become a serious question.

The story grew as it was told over and over again. David became a hero only second to Hoppo himself. It became the accepted view that he had taught the monkey to steal the mate's hat and then had made him throw it overboard. The incident made him popular among the foremast hands — but not with Mr. Starbuck.

So went the voyage of the Sea Turtle as the little whaler

gradually drew near Cape Horn. Her crew carried on their regular routine and still found plenty of time to spend long hours spinning their endless yarns. David worked in the galley. Every day was like the day before. The excitement of chasing whales for which the boy had shipped seemed to be as unlikely as if he stayed at home.

The weather, which had so far been favorable in every way, gradually began to change, however, and it was not so very long after the monkey chase that heavy seas rolling up from the south began to make difficult going for the Sea Turtle. The crew wondered whether Captain Hunter would not have to lay to for a while before trying to get around Cape Horn if conditions did not moderate. But he held the ship to her course. He was not the man to be afraid of a stiff blow and the southern voyage had taken so long that he was anxious to get to the Pacific grounds as soon as possible. After all, it was a business voyage on which they were engaged, and you couldn't get oil without finding the whales first.

For two days the Sea Turtle now fought against head winds, cold, biting blasts of air from the frozen continent to the south which kicked up the sea and whined bleakly through the shrouds. It was a far different state of affairs from that which had prevailed in those calm days when David had been lulled to sleep by the ship's gentle motion and the sun's comfortable warmth. Tremendous seas continually broke over the Sea Turtle's blunt little prow and swept across her broad deck. A man's life was not worth much if he found himself out of reach of something to which he could cling for support. Sail had to be shortened; the watch on deck was ordered aloft to take in canvas. But Captain Hunter kept as much sail on his ship as he dared, and drove her for all she was worth.

After one such day David was sleeping fitfully in his bunk when suddenly awakened about midnight.

'All hands on deck!' rang out Mr. Starbuck's shouted order above the howling of the wind. 'Tumble out, you watch below! Tumble out! All hands!'

The boy slid from his bunk and hurriedly grabbed his boots and oilskins. The Sea Turtle was pitching fearfully. In the inky blackness of the forecastle, for the swinging lamp had gone out, it was easy to imagine that the vessel must be in imminent danger. The pounding of the sea against her sides and the ominous creaking of her timbers seemed to foreshadow disaster. There was a heavy list to port and as some unusually heavy sea crashed against the little ship, she would quiver from stem to stern. David felt trapped, imprisoned, in the shut-in forecastle. Of the grumbling, cursing seamen struggling into their oilskins, he was the first to crawl up the ladder and make his way on deck.

He was almost swept off his feet as he emerged from the hatchway. The night was a pitiless black, the rain sweeping down in chill torrents, and such a gale raging that it seemed impossible that the Sea Turtle could weather it.

'Furl the mizzen topsail!' shouted a voice almost in David's ear as he clung desperately to the rail.

The boy was suddenly afraid. He couldn't face going aloft on such a night when every blast of wind seemed about to tear him from the ship, and when blinded by the rain he could not see a foot in front of him. But at the mate's order the men had staggered over to the rigging and were painfully groping their way aloft. David gulped and blindly followed them.

How he made his way to the yardarm, he did not know. The wind roared through the rigging more fiercely than ever, the sails tore at their fastenings, and the mast swayed dizzily back and forth. Now he seemed to be about to be plunged into the very depths of the sea, now he was carried skyward in a surging sweep. Only once did he dare look below. He could not see the deck. It was an eerie, horrifying feeling. His feet slipped as he felt his way out along the icy yard, grasping frantically with benumbed fingers at anything on which he could get a grip.

Suddenly through the night, above the roar of the storm and the howling of the wind, came a piercing shriek.

'Oh, my God!'...

The terror-struck boy sensed rather than saw a dark form shoot through the air so close to him that it almost swept him off in its downward fall. He clung desperately to the yard, his feet swaying, as at that moment the Sea Turtle buried her nose in the sea and an immense wave swept across her deck with a crash of splintering wood. One of the whaleboats was stove; the masts themselves seemed likely to be jumped out any moment.

'Man overboard! Man overboard!' came a faint shout from below.

But nothing could be done. No boat could be lowered in that sea. If one were, it could not last a moment. The Sea Turtle herself was at the mercy of the elements. Forces far beyond the control of her crew were mocking at their efforts to take in sail. But it had to be done. Otherwise her masts would surely go or she would be thrown on her beam ends. There would be time later to discover who had been swept overboard, that is, if the ship lived through the night.

Sail had to be taken in. David was struggling against the terrific pull of the canvas when he realized the man next to him was shouting in his ear.

'Somebody's got to take that poor devil's place!' the seaman yelled. 'Somebody's got to help with the topsail.'

The boy looked up. Could he move from where he **was**? If he had to do it, by graminy, he could do it.

Shutting his eyes, David edged in along the yard, climbed farther up those madly swaying shrouds, and crept out to where the fallen seaman had lost his footing but a few moments before. But he was too late. With a report like a pistol shot, the sail was wrenched free of its fastenings and in another second torn to ribbons. The boy threw himself over the yard and clung there grimly.

Nothing more could be done. What sails could be taken in, the crew had furled; the others had been ripped to shreds. The Sea Turtle was now scudding before the wind beneath bare poles. The men aloft climbed gingerly down. Never in all his life had David felt such a feeling of relief as when his feet again touched deck. The ship was still pitching madly, the wind shaking her as a terrier shakes a rat, but in comparison with the dizzy sweeps of the masthead, the deck felt solid and secure.

The boy stood for a while, holding on to a stay, and watched the dark masses of water breaking over the Sea Turtle's bow. He was cold and wet. The driving rain beat upon his face and the wind tore at his oilskin. But safely back on deck, he exulted in the storm. The frantic pitching of the vessel no longer concerned him, and somehow he felt sure that the Sea Turtle would ride out the gale whatever happened.

'That was good work aloft there. You've the makin's of a sailor in you, lad.'

David started. Captain Hunter, making his way forward to look over the damage caused by the wave which had swept away the whaleboat, loomed up out of the dark.

'Thank you, sir,' the boy answered, but his words were swept away by the wind. Captain Hunter went on.

David felt a thrill of satisfaction. The makings of a sailor! Perhaps he'd get out of the galley after all. As on that first night leaving New Bedford, he welcomed the rush of wind and spray on his chilled face.

VII

THE SEA TURTLE STOPS FOR MAIL

Turtle Race

Chapter VII

IT WAS several days before the Sea Turtle, with new sails to replace those she had lost, was finally able to beat her way about Cape Horn. Although the storm somewhat abated after that first night, bad weather continued and only the most skillful seamanship enabled the vessel to resume her course toward the Pacific. Not until almost a week later, when the deep swells of that ocean at last succeeded the mountainous seas which broke upon the Cape, did Captain Hunter find an opportunity to read the burial service in memory of the man lost overboard.

David had felt badly when he had learned later on that night of storm that the lost sailor was one of his watch, a young fellow about his own age with whom he had been on the friendliest terms. That very afternoon they had been talking together about why they had come whaling. Now he was gone. It brought home to the boy as could nothing else the perils and hazards of the long voyage on which he had embarked. As Captain Hunter read the solemn words of the burial service, with the entire crew gathered in the ship's waist, he wondered whether he would ever see his home and family again.

But it was not his nature to remain discouraged for very long, and now that Captain Hunter had praised him, he felt more confident of everything about the voyage. He did not really believe that he would fall from the masthead or be washed overboard; he did not really believe he would be kept in the galley when they lowered after whales. Reaching the Pacific seemed to him a symbol of good luck.

'How soon is there a chance of sighting whales?' he asked Frank one day as the two sat together on the windlass lazily watching the Sea Turtle plough through the sea.

'There's no tellin',' the harpooner answered. 'Not for a while yet, though. Of course when *you're* lookout, we expect to see 'em any time, but we got to reach the grounds first.'

'Where are the grounds?'

'Oh, they're out there in the Pacific.' Frank waved his hand vaguely in the direction the Sea Turtle was heading. 'We'll probably try the on-shore grounds first. Then if we have no luck, we'll sail westward to the off-shore grounds, out in mid-ocean, before heading up north toward Hawaii and Japan. That's what we usually do.'

'Do you always find whales at the grounds?'

'Not always. You can't ever tell. I've known a ship to cruise six months, tacking back and forth every day and lying-to every night, and not sight a spout. Then I've known 'em raise so many whales, and kill 'em, that the try-pots were goin' night and day. You can't count on fisherman's luck.'

'Gosh, I hope we lower soon!' David exclaimed impulsively. 'I'd like to see a whale. I'm beginning to believe there aren't any.'

'I've seen 'em thick as minnows in a bait pail,' Frank said. 'I remember one time we ran right smack into a whole school of spermaceti. We couldn't hardly lower a boat without landing on one of 'em. The Old Man tried throwing a harpoon from the bowsprit, and danged if he didn't get fast with his first iron. What a day that was!'

Frank sighed mournfully and looked down at the little piece of bone which he was carefully carving with his jack-knife. He was a past-master at that form of carving called by the whalemen scrimshawing, and the bone he now held in his huge hand was being slowly and delicately turned into a little model of a whaleboat. For some time he bent closely over his work.

'What happened? What happened?' David at last asked impatiently.

'What happened? You mean about that whale? He was a big fellow, must have been an eighty-barreler. I've never seen such a whale.'

'Did you catch him?'

'Sure we caught him. We caught him all right. But he got away.

'You see it was this way. When the Old Man saw that his harpoon was buried good and deep in that crittur, he quickly took a loop about the capstan with his line. But did it bother that whale to be tied to a full-rigged ship? It did not. He started off towin' the ship behind him just as if she was a whaleboat. What's more, he headed straight into the wind.

'We had all sails set and it didn't make a rap of difference. He was towin' us against the wind about as fast as we ever sailed with it. The harpoon held and we had him neat as could be so soon as he got a bit tired, but the trouble was he didn't get tired. He tore along like I don't know what, stirrin' up a regular tidal wave in his wake. He kept it up all day, and every once and a while he seemed to look back at us and grin. At least that's what it looked like.

'Finally, the Old Man begins to get sort of nervous. He was pacin' up and down the quarterdeck swearin' like a trooper. But there warn't a thing he could do. You can't pull up on a whale when he's towin' a ship against the wind at about two knots. What really worried the Old Man, though, was that he was headed toward Cape Horn. If we'd had a full ship, that might have been all right, but we'd only just got to the whaling grounds. It looked as if he'd have to cut the line or ...'

Just then a cry of 'Land ho!' rang out from the lookout stationed on the mainmast.

David jumped up and saw on the horizon a faint speck.

'What is it? What is it?' he demanded excitedly, completely forgetting Frank's story.

'Yes, sir,' he heard the harpooner saying, going on as if nothing had happened aboard the Sea Turtle, 'it was cut the line, or be hauled all the way back to New Bedford. That whale seemed to have taken a notion into his head to go somewhere. So the Old Man sings out, "Cut the line!" and I cut the line. The minute the whale feels the ship is no longer fast, he stops in his tracks, by way of speakin'. Then he swims slowly toward us and comes so close we can see the wrinkles on his forehead. They're all crinkly-like. The dodgasted whale was laughing at us. As sure as my name's Frank White, he was laughing at us. After a while...'

'That's a grand story, Frank, a grand story,' David interrupted, 'But listen: is that an island or something — there, that land off the port bow?'

Frank at last looked up.

'Sure it's an island. What in blazes did you think it was? Europe? Or a whale? It's one of the Galapagos Islands. I guess we're goin' to stop there for mail.'

The big sailor carefully smoothed off the sharp-pointed bow of the little boat he was carving out of whalebone, got up slowly, and with a grin at the mystified boy lumbered off. David stared after him. What did he mean — mail? Frank was filling him full of a lot of wild yarns. He couldn't believe anything he told him after that story about a whale towing a ship. He saw the blacksmith on the other side of the deck and decided to try to get more authentic information.

'Say, Tim,' he asked the old man, 'are we going to stop at that island?'

'I guess so,' came the surprising answer. 'Every whaler calls at Galapagos post-office some time or other.'

The island was now close enough so that David could see that its rocky shores gave not the slightest sign of human habitation. Mail? Post-office? But since Frank and Tim were in agreement, he thought it better to ask no more questions. He would wait and see what happened.

A few hours later the Sea Turtle lay at anchor off a stretch of beach which for a short distance lined the island's rocky shore. It did not look too inviting — there were none of those tropical palms filled with monkeys which made up David's picture of islands in the Pacific — but nevertheless the boy was intensely anxious to get ashore if he could. When Captain Hunter gave the order to lower two boats, he waited in fearful suspense. Mr. Starbuck showed no sign of taking him, and for a time he was sure he would be left aboard ship again. Then Captain Hunter himself noticed the disappointed boy and with a jerk of his thumb ordered him to go with Mr. Macy. David needed no urging. He jumped to the gunwale, and, sliding down the falls, dropped into the second mate's boat.

It took an exciting pull through the breakers before the

boat could be beached, but the moment its bow touched land David was over the side. He could hardly wait to help draw the craft up on shore before he was off, running up and down the beach in the sheer joy of being on land again. He had forgotten what it was to feel something firmer than the Sea Turtle's deck under foot. He had forgotten the look of sand and trees and rocks. He had forgotten the earthy smell of the land, and a nose too accustomed to salt air sniffed eagerly at the breeze which caught up the odor of green, growing things.

An unexpected order brought him suddenly back to reality.

'Here, there!' Mr. Macy was shouting. 'Since you're so full of energy, lug this along.'

David had almost forgotten what he had heard about the purpose of the Sea Turtle's call at this island, but it came back to him as he caught the object which Mr. Macy tossed to him. It was a mail pouch, apparently full of letters and newspapers. Slinging it over his shoulder, the boy followed the mate toward a high rocky point which jutted out to sea.

After climbing for some time they found themselves in an open space where stood a curious object such as David had never seen before. It looked exactly like the shell of a turtle, but was almost five feet long.

'Give me a hand here.'

Mr. Macy was trying to turn the thing over. The boy hurried over to help and together they pushed it to one side, uncovering quite a pile of pouches similar to the one David had been carrying.

'There won't be anything for us,' the mate muttered half to himself, glancing into one or two of the pouches. 'But we'll leave our stuff.'

David could contain himself no longer.

'What's this thing, sir?' he asked, kicking the shell. 'Where did all these letters come from? I don't understand.'

Mr. Macy laughed.

'Didn't you know we whalemen had a post-office here? Regular mail service. Not every day, perhaps; maybe every year. But special delivery just the same. But you asked me two questions.

'This thing's just what it looks like. It's the shell of a tortoise, a giant tortoise. He weighed about — well, I'd say three hundred pounds, before he became a mail box. I guess these fellows grow larger here on Galapagos than anywhere else in the world. You'll see some of 'em. We'll be taking a few back to the ship. You don't have to feed 'em and they'll live on shipboard for months. They make good steak.

'Now where'd these letters come from? Just as you see. We brought a batch. Every whaleship coming around Cape Horn stops at the Galapagos Islands. Even if they haven't any letters for other ships, they leave the papers. We're fresh from home; we don't care. But suppose some ship comes by which has been away three years. Her crew will be mighty anxious to see if any letters have been left for 'em and to get a chance to look over some papers and find out what's been happening in the world since they left port.'

David was listening with interest to Mr. Macy's explanation when an idea suddenly struck him.

'Maybe I could find out something about my uncle,' he exclaimed. 'Perhaps there's a letter he left here to be taken home or something.'

'Your uncle?'

'Yes, Captain Bob Worth. He sailed aboard the Rover. It's a long time now. His ship's not been heard from for more than two years.'

'Captain Bob Worth. No, I guess I don't know him. You say nobody's spoke the Rover for over two years. That's a funny thing. That harpooner called Dago Jack was saying something about the Rover the other day.'

'He was?'

David was startled. It was some time since he had thought about further trying to identify Dago Jack with the Portuguese in Uncle Bob's story. He had steered clear of him as much as possible. But if Dago Jack had once sailed on the Rover, he was surely the man. Could he know anything about what had happened to his uncle? That seemed impossible. It would probably have been an earlier voyage.

'Yes, I think he said he'd sailed on the Rover,' Mr. Macy went on, 'but I don't know whether your uncle was in command. When was she last spoken?'

'I don't know,' David answered. 'There were stories... Look at this!'

While they had been talking, the boy had been rummaging through some of the mail and he now held in his hand a soiled and tattered letter which was addressed in bold, irregular handwriting to Abner Worth.

'By graminy, that's my father!' he exclaimed. 'It must be from Uncle Bob.'

He hurriedly tore it open and started reading.

Dear Abner [he read] I'm sending this by Captain Holden of the Fairhaven. I hope it will reach you. We've had a poor voyage so far. Little oil and a mutinous crew. I'm going to keep them working until we get a full ship whatever happens, and am now bound to the Fiji Islands. Spoke the Fairhaven off Pitt Island. Today is July 15, 1845, and we ought to be home early next year. Tell David I'll take him out my next voyage if he still wants to come whaling. Your brother, Bob.

David's hand was trembling as he finished the short note. He stared thoughtfully out to sea.

'That's about two years ago,' he said, almost to himself. 'I wonder how the letter got here instead of being brought home by Captain Holden. What could have happened? He was sailing for the Fiji Islands — and a mutinous crew.'

'There's no telling, David,' Mr. Macy answered kindly. 'That's a long time. He might have been shipwrecked. His ship might have been captured by natives. Those Fiji Islanders aren't always so friendly. Maybe it was mutiny.'

'There was a story about mutiny,' said the boy. 'Gosh, I wonder if Uncle Bob may not be somewhere, held by savages or on a deserted island. We might rescue him.'

Mr. Macy gave the boy a fatherly pat on the shoulder.

'There's not much chance of that. But we'll see if we can pick up any news of the Rover whenever we speak another whaleship, or if we put into any of the islands. It sometimes takes a long time for news to get around in the whaling fleet. But you better forget about it, lad, and make yourself into a good whaleman to take your uncle's place. Come along now, it's about time to be getting back to the boat.'

David stuffed the letter in his pocket and after they had carefully put the great tortoise shell back over the mail pouches, the two of them started back toward the shore.

As they drew near a part of the beach which they had gone around on climbing up to the post-office, they were confronted with an amazing spectacle. The shore was crowded with huge tortoises, many of them fully as big as the one whose shell served as a mail box, and a group of excited seamen were prodding them with sticks in a frantic attempt to drive them over to the beached whaleboats.

As David drew near, Frank spied him.

'Here, you farmer!' he called out gleefully. 'Here's a chance to see what you can do. Let's see how you can drive a tortoise. If we can get a few of these fellows into the boats, we'll have fresh meat for months. Come on. I want to see a farm boy drive one of these gallumpin' Galapagos terrapin.'

Grabbing a stick, the boy joined in the fun. It was hard work to get those tortoises to move. The sailors would no more than get one started in the right direction than he would laboriously start turning around or else stop dead. Even when by dint of constant work they could keep one going in the right direction, progress was so slow that it seemed as if it would take them hours to get anywhere near the boats.

'Let's have a race!' shouted Frank.

Jumping on the back of one of the tortoises which he had been vainly prodding from the rear, he belabored its heavy shell with resounding whacks. David quickly followed suit and with legs astride urged on his dozing steed as if he were riding on the back of an ox.

'Come on, there, old stick-in-the-mud!' he shouted. 'Stir a leg, will you? Git up! Git up! Hump along with you! That's more like it. Come on, old molasses, come on! Hey! He's dyin' under me! Git up! Git up!'

It was no use. Frank's tortoise was moving slowly shoreward, but for all the boy could do, his steed would not budge an inch. Hard as he thumped its shell, loudly as he shouted at it, the lethargic animal would not stir. David stood up and, carefully balancing, tried jumping up and down on its back. Even that did not help.

'You win!' David called after Frank. 'You win!'

With a final whack at the tortoise, the boy jumped to the ground. No sooner was he off than the tortoise stuck out its head and started crawling, at amazing speed, toward the shore line.

For almost an hour the seamen played with the tortoises, but it was soon evident that at that rate they would never get any of them into the boats. Then someone suggested hauling them with a whaleline. One was quickly brought, tied to one of the animals by a loop about its shell, and eight men dragged it across the sand. It took a great deal of heaving and pulling to get the tortoise into the boat, but at last this was done. Another was then dragged down to the second boat. With about five hundred pounds of turtle promising several steak dinners, the two boats finally put off and returned triumphantly to the Sea Turtle.

VIII

DAGO JACK STIRS UP TROUBLE

The Toe of the First Mate's Boot

Chapter VIII

FOR several days David had noticed that wherever Dago Jack went, he left behind him a trail of discontent among the members of the Sea Turtle's crew.

He had made it his own policy, ever since the first days of the voyage, to stay away from the Portuguese just as much as possible. While he was working in the galley, this had been very easy. But when Captain Hunter relieved him of this assignment, shortly after the night of the storm about Cape Horn, the boy had found himself subject to Dago Jack's orders whenever Mr. Starbuck put the harpooner in charge of some work involving his watch. There was no question that he still bore the boy a grudge. David would be told to scrub the deck when it was really the task of some other member of the crew, or he would be ordered to help the cook despite his official release from the galley.

It was not anything personal, however, which now aroused David's suspicions as to Dago Jack's actions. He often saw him in deep and serious conversation with Spider. Whenever anyone drew near, they would draw apart. Then there was one other man whom the Portuguese had apparently singled out for his confidences. He was a surly, dull-witted German who boasted a great deal about what he had done on previous voyages, but was always shirking his work aboard the Sea Turtle and grumbling about the officers. He was called 'Hungry Heinie' because he ate more than any other two men in the crew.

One night, after a long, slow day, a group had gathered about the windlass and were gloomily talking about what hard luck the Sea Turtle had had. She had not raised a single whale since she had left New Bedford.

'She's an unlucky ship.'

The voice came out of the darkness. No one had noticed that Dago Jack was standing there. Everyone turned toward him.

'What do you mean?' one of the green hands asked.

'Ever since Captain Hunter's had her,' Dago Jack answered, 'she's been unlucky. Last voyage she was out four years, and then came home only partly full. She lost four men; six others took sick.'

'What do you know about it?' someone asked sharply. 'You didn't ship aboard her.'

'I heard about her, though. About half the crew deserted at Valparaiso. They said she was hoodoo-ed. It was a funny thing about such hard luck and so many men gettin' sick.'

'I feel sort of sick myself,' interjected Heinie. 'I don't ever get enough to eat...'

A roar of laughter greeted this comment, but Heinie went doggedly on.

'What do we get to eat? A lot of salt junk, so tough you'd break an axe on it, and ship's biscuit so full of maggots it's ready to walk off. What's happened to that tortoise steak we were going to have? We get about one bite and the rest goes to the cabin. I tell you, Captain Hunter's so afraid he won't get oil that he's goin' to starve us to make up for it.'

'Oh, cut your jawin', Heinie,' interposed the sailor who had taken Dago Jack to task. 'The grub's good enough and it ain't the Old Man's fault if we don't sight whales. We got nothin' to complain about yet.'

The conversation continued for some time and always Dago Jack, Heinie, or Spider was ready with some slighting remark about the ship's hard luck, the food, the sharp manner of Captain Hunter, or Mr. Starbuck's rough-and-ready discipline. David was not the only member of the crew to have felt the toe of the first mate's boot. He had once sent Spider sprawling halfway across the deck when he had made an insolent reply to an order. Even though most of the crew seemed ready to take whatever happened as a matter of course, there was no doubt the talk of the three malcontents made some impression on them.

It was not altogether surprising. The monotony of life on shipboard strained the nerves of both officers and men. When day after day passed without sight or sign of whales, it was not hard to believe that either the Sea Turtle or Captain Hunter was ill-starred. The foremast hands had too much time to think. Make sail, man the mastheads, scrub the decks; breakfast, dinner, supper; shorten sail, boats' crew drill, and turn-in! That was all there was to it. And every day exactly the same as the day before. David felt the discontent, sensed the quarrelsomeness of men on whose hands time hung too heavily.

Nor could it be said that the food aboard the Sea Turtle was appetizing. At first it had not seemed so bad, but the deadly sameness of it became almost unendurable. There was always pork, beans and corn on Monday, codfish and potatoes on Tuesday, and mush and beef on Wednesday. Then Thursday brought pork and beans again, Friday meant beef and rice, and Saturday was another round of codfish and potatoes. Only on Sunday was there any addition to this staple diet of salt junk and dried vegetables. Duff was served for dinner. But Sam had a heavy hand and it might better have been omitted. Also the biscuit was always maggoty and the weak liquid, which Sam one day called tea and the next day coffee, tasted like dishwater.

If there had been a chance to lower after whales, if anything had happened to break the dull routine of the seemingly endless cruising, the men would not have minded the food. They would not have paid any attention to such grumblers as Dago Jack and his henchmen. But under the circumstances, they began to think that perhaps they were being badly treated and that in some one way or another the officers were responsible for everything which went wrong. Every day saw their dissatisfaction deepen, their mood become more quarrelsome.

Finally the storm broke.

It was a calm, hot day. The Sea Turtle was barely moving in a sea as flat as pancake. The men lying dully about the deck, idly yarning or patching away on their old clothes, showed hardly a flicker of interest when at noon Sam sang out to them to come and get their grub. Two or three of them finally got to their feet and wandered over to the galley to collect the two kids in which their salt pork and dried beans had been ladled out.

For a time nothing was heard as with sheath knife or fingers the foremast hands dished out what they wanted and dipped their tin cups into the steaming bucket of tea.

'Now in the name of my uncle's stepfather,' one man suddenly called out in a bitter voice, 'what in heck is this?'

He held out his sheath knife with something dark on its point.

'Why, it's a bit of Sam's shoe,' another seaman growled. 'What do yer think we've been gettin' these days? Meat? That all goes to the cabin. You're goldarned lucky to have a bit of rope or leather. What's this dodgasted thing?'

He in turn held up a strange object stuck on the end of his knife.

'See that? See that? That's what that good-fer-nothin' sea cook who sleeps in the galley says is ship's biscuit. Yea, he calls it ship biscuit, the lazy, black scoundrel. I couldn't even have got it stuck on my knife if I hadn't pounded the handle with a belayin' pin. The point's busted at that. They wouldn't have it in the cabin, I'll bet. Oh, no. But it's good enough fer us. We don't know better. We've got cast-iron jaws and like to chaw on rocks.'

'What are you growlin' about?' broke in Frank good-naturedly. 'Do you expect a bloomin' porterhouse when you're on a whaleship? Do you expect a biscuit to taste like a piece of cake?'

'Taste? How can I taste this hunk of hardtack? If I tried to bite it, I'd break every durned tooth in my head. I'll bounce it off Sam's head, that's what I'll do with the blamed thing.'

'Soak it in your tea and it'll loosen up a bit.'

'Soak it in my tea, you say. That's a fine idea! Soak it in my tea, and fill that up with dirty maggots. I got a right to decent food and I'm not goin' to break my teeth for anyone. I'll be hornswoggled if I am.'

'That's right! By golly, he's right,' Heinie broke in. 'I told you, didn't I? They're eatin' cakes in the cabin and givin' us this dirty truck. They're tryin' to starve us. That's what they're tryin' to do.'

'What about the salt junk? That's what I want to know,

by cripes. If anybody wants to eat the sort of stuff Sam's
boilin' up and callin' beef, he can have his belly full for all I
care. But you heard about the men gettin' sick on the last
voyage? I won't do it. No, by golly, and I don't care who
knows it. No more parboiled shoes for me.'

With a sudden gesture Heinie threw the contents of his
plate over the ship's side and looked around belligerently.

'What about it, mates?'

There was a growl of assent. For a moment no one stirred.
Then with an oath Dago Jack hurled his plate overboard. As
if he had released a spring, the seamen leaped to their feet,
flinging their food over the rail. With angry curses they drew
together in a close knot in the waist of the ship and waited for
someone to take the lead as to what should be done next.

David had listened to this outburst in amazement. He
found the food no better than did anyone else. But what
could be done about it? Was this revolt going to help
matters? What would happen next?

It was Spider who noticed that his plate was still heaped
with pork and beans.

'Cripes!' he shouted. 'Look at him, will yer? What do
you think you're doin', you mother's pet! Goin' up to the
quarterdeck and report that you're a good boy and like old
shoes and maggoty hardtack? No, you don't.'

With a swift kick he sent David's plate whirling over the
rail.

'We stick together in this, see? You don't like this stinkin'
truck any better than the rest of us, see? If you do, I'll show
you!'

He thrust his ugly face menacingly toward the boy, but before David had a chance to answer, someone else spoke up.

'I tell you what we'll do. The boy can go up to the quarter-

deck and tell 'em just where we stand. We want better food
and we're goin' to have it. Not another lick of work out of us,
by crackity, until we get what we want. The boy can make a
good speech. But by all that's holy, if he don't talk straight,
I'll lambast the tar out of him myself. If he don't play fair,
his mother won't know him when I'm finished.'

David looked around quickly. It occurred to him that this
wasn't just what Dago Jack had expected, but his shipmates
were muttering their approval of the suggestion. It seemed
clear he would have to be their spokesman whether Dago
Jack wanted it or not. He started reluctantly toward the
quarterdeck.

Captain Hunter came out of the cabin. He gave one look
at the men sullenly gathered in the waist. With his chin set
determinedly, he turned fiercely on the terrified boy.

'Well?'

'I'm sorry, sir,' David began weakly. 'You see the crew —
I mean, us — we feel we aren't getting our rightful rations.
They want — I mean, we want — more meat and the bis-
cuit's so hard...'

His voice trailed away miserably. He couldn't face
Captain Hunter's stony glare. He didn't know what to say;
didn't know what to do.

After a second's pause Captain Hunter turned away and
stepped back into the cabin companionway. When he re-
appeared, almost instantly, he held a cat-o'-nine-tails in his
hand, a piece of knotted rope whose significance no one could
misunderstand.

Disregarding David entirely, he looked down at the crew.
'So you don't like your food?'

He hardly raised his voice, but his menacing tone carried
clearly to the men foregathered in the waist. They shifted

about uneasily, refusing to meet his penetrating glance. David stood as if rooted to the spot, his eyes fixed fearfully on the sinister-looking cat-o'-nine-tails.

'So you don't like your food? You've sent this boy aft to complain. You want roast beef and mince pie. You want cake, I suppose. By the great horn spoon, what in blazes do you think this is, a Sunday School picnic?'

'I won't have any insubordination aboard this ship, you understand? I'll string up every man of you and give you a taste of this' — shaking the cat-o'-nine-tails — 'and discharge you at the next port. You're gettin' good food and plenty of it. Has anybody got anything to say further? Speak up, now. Speak up!'

No one of the sailors moved. As Captain Hunter stood there facing them, with both Mr. Starbuck and Mr. Macy just behind him, not a sound broke the stillness which had fallen over the Sea Turtle except the gentle lapping of the water at her prow. Not a man stirred.

'Do you hear me?' Captain Hunter roared. 'What have you got to say?'

He glared down at them. Mr. Starbuck was clenching and unclenching his hands angrily; Mr. Macy looked unhappy.

Finally Heinie stepped forward.

'We can't eat this salt junk,' he said defiantly. 'It's not fit to eat. We're agreed on it and we won't work ship...'

'What do you say? You won't work ship!'

Captain Hunter grew purple with suppressed fury.

'By God, that's mutiny. You know what that means? I'll teach you to tell me what my crew's goin' to do. Come here!'

There was a sudden movement in the waist. But no one stepped forward. Rather the crew closed in about their spokesman. Dago Jack had been standing somewhat aloof, keeping himself, as a boatsteerer, apart from the foremast hands. He now glanced quickly toward the racks on which stood the harpoons, the lances, the cutting-in spades of the whaler's gear, and whispered something to Spider. If Captain Hunter noticed it, he gave no sign.

'Mr. Starbuck' — the sharp order cut the air like a knife — 'bring that man here.'

With belligerent eagerness the first mate stepped forward and in a few quick strides was among the men. Not a hand was raised against him, but the little knot about Heinie drew closer together. Mr. Starbuck pushed them roughly aside.

'Come along with you!' he ordered peremptorily, and grabbed the man by the shoulder with a cruel grip. 'Come along with you!'

Heinie stubbornly refused to budge.

'Take that, then!'

Mr. Starbuck released his hold on the man's shoulder and, drawing back his arm, planted a blow on the side of Heinie's head which sent him crashing to the deck.

'You asked for it, and you got it.'

Mr. Starbuck spoke quietly, but there was a steely ring in his voice as he stepped back and looked, not at the prostrate form of the sailor whom he had felled, but at his sullen shipmates. Still no one moved and the Sea Turtle sailed on in an ominous quiet.

'All right, Mr. Starbuck,' came the icy voice of Captain Hunter. 'Have that man put in irons and send the crew forward to their own quarters.'

'Forward where you belong,' the mate ordered.

'We won't stand for it.'

No one could say who started it. But almost instinctively

the men fell back to where the whaling weapons stood in the racks. Calloused hands reached back to grasp the sharpened irons; blunt fingers closed around the shafts...

Just then a shrill cry rang out from the masthead:

'There she blows! She blows! She blo——ows!'

IX

THERE SHE BLOWS!

Harpooning

Chapter IX

'THERE she blows! She blows! She blo——ows!'
The movement of the crew toward the whaling weapons was halted as quickly as it had started. Not a single member of the crew, not even Dago Jack, could resist the imperative summons of that long-awaited call. As the lookout repeated his frenzied shout and pointed excitedly off the port bow, the threatened mutiny was forgotten. The Sea Turtle's crew was dramatically recalled to the objective of their voyage: the pursuit of whales.

Mr. Starbuck was the first to rush to the rail and look off eagerly in the direction in which the lookout was pointing. Within a few seconds, every man had either followed him or was climbing up the ratlines to get a still better view. Heinie was left alone lying on the deck, the only evidence that there had been trouble between officers and crew.

David had at first been too startled to move, but once it dawned upon him that whales had really been raised, he too was eagerly making his way aloft. A thrilling sight met his eyes. Off the port bow, not more than a mile, were whales. Not one whale, not two or three, but a whole school of them.

They were rolling carelessly in the long swells, sending up

huge geysers of misty air from their spout-holes, geysers
which broke over their broad backs in dazzling cascades.
One huge fellow rose suddenly to the surface and threw himself out of the water, tumbling back with a resounding splash
which could be heard aboard the Sea Turtle. They were
sperm whales, as their single spouts proved, and some of them
looked gigantic. The amazing spectacle of their playing
there on the surface of the sea held David fascinated.

But there was no time to watch them.

'Get ready to lower!' shouted Captain Hunter.

'Mr. Starbuck, take the starboard boat. Mr. Macy, stay
with the ship. I'll lower myself. Jump to it! Spring, my
lads, spring!'

'Aye, aye, sir.'

The men jumped to it with alacrity. There was a rush to
the boats. No thought of quarreling or complaining now. No
thought of anything but whales. The order to lower boats!
This was why they had come to sea. The spirit of the chase
transformed the atmosphere aboard the Sea Turtle as could
nothing else. As David ran to where the bow boat hung on its
davits, he forgot everything that had happened in the exciting prospect which lay before him.

Dago Jack was already in the boat looking over his whaling
gear and making sure that everything was shipshape in the
little craft. The boat crew was busily making ready to lower.
It was not until he was about to jump into the boat himself
that David suddenly remembered that he was only spare
man in this crew. He had no regular berth. There would be
no need for him that day. Disappointment struck him so
forcibly that he could almost have wept.

'Ready?'

'Aye, aye, sir!'

'Lower away!'

At Captain Hunter's command the men let go the falls and three boats dropped simultaneously into the water. Heedlessly their crews slid down the ropes after them or jumped from the rail to fall sprawling on the thwarts. In another moment they had seized their oars, and, shoving off from the vessel's side at the boatheaders' orders, dug in for the pull to where the whales were still sporting in the long Pacific rollers. David stood dejectedly by the rail.

He was still watching the boats when to his surprise one of them turned back. It was Mr. Starbuck's, and from the mate's angry gesticulations, the boy realized that something had gone wrong. So did Mr. Macy, left aboard as shipkeeper, and he hurried over to the rail.

'This club-footed son-of-a-sea-cook can't pull an oar!' shouted Mr. Starbuck, jerking his finger toward the bow oarsman and swearing vehemently. 'If I don't get another man, we'll be swamped before we're half a mile from the ship. If I ever saw such a clumsy, hornswoggled, deadbeat...'

Mr. Macy looked over toward the little group of seamen left aboard ship and was about to order one of them into Mr. Starbuck's boat when he caught sight of David.

'Can you do it, lad?' he asked quietly.

'Yes, sir. I'm sure I can. I'm sure!' David answered eagerly.

He was not sure. Now that he had a chance to take part in the chase, he was dreadfully afraid he would somehow boggle it. But this was his opportunity. Not for anything in the world would he pass it up.

'Yes, sir,' he repeated. 'I can do it.'

'All right, jump for it.'

David needed no further word. As the returning boat

swung alongside the ship and the discomfited bow oarsman started to clamber out, the boy jumped from the rail and landed in a heap in the bottom of the boat.

'What are you doing here?' Mr. Starbuck asked angrily when he saw who his new oarsman was. 'Mr. Macy, is that the best you can do for me? He'll be no better than the fool I had before.'

There was no time to change again, however, and making the best of it the first mate ordered the boy to take his place. The boat was shoved off for a second time and with David manfully pulling his heavy oar, they set off in pursuit of the other boats, now far ahead of them.

Steering with the long sweep braced against his leg, Mr. Starbuck swore fiercely at his straining crew. The five men pulled for all they were worth, but it was hard to make up the big lead which the other boats had. The mate blamed them for being so far behind, and each time he started on a new tirade of abuse, he especially singled out David.

The boy was doing the best he could. But soon his hands were blistered, his muscles sore and strained, and his back seemed about to break. It was the hardest work he had ever tried in his life. He could not see where the boat was going. He could not see anything but the thick neck of the man in front of him. The boat was speeding through the water at a fast clip, cleaving a swift furrow through the sea, but whether the whales were anywhere in sight, whether they had sounded or whether they were still on the surface, David had not the slightest idea.

He would have given almost anything in the world for a quick look over his shoulder. But he did not dare make any such move. There was nothing to do but pull on the heavy oar, however much his hands and back might hurt. And pull he did. He was determined to make good. Mr. Starbuck would have no chance to say that he had shirked or not been able to do his part.

'Get into it! Get into it!' the mate was shouting. 'You bow oarsman, I'd like to get my hands on you. Pull, won't ye? Oh, my stars and cuttle fishes, what's the matter with you all? Pull! Pull! You dunderheads! Can't you do any better than that? You'd think the boat was stuck! You'd think we were towing a whale! Spring, you landlubbers; spring, you jackanapes! For the love of your grandmothers, won't ye pull? We're after whales! We're after oil! Pull, boys, pull!'

The boat was making fast time. It had almost caught up to the others. David still had no idea of what might have happened to the whales, but from the rising excitement in Mr. Starbuck's voice, he thought they must be getting close to them. He could almost imagine that he heard them wallowing alongside. When the spray broke over the bow in a drenching shower of salt water, he was sure it must be from a whale's spout. He thought he could smell a whale.

He was still afraid to look over his shoulder. He knew that if he did, Mr. Starbuck would about kill him. It was his business, it was the business of every man in the boat, to pull. There was no time to worry about anything else. He bent to his oar and, with the sweat pouring down his face and blinding his eyes, struggled to keep up his end in this frantic race to reach the whales before they sounded.

They were close to them. There could be no doubt about it. It was in the air. The water was churned up all about them and it seemed as if they must be in the middle of the school. David half expected to have a whale jump into the boat. Then he realized that if one so much as flicked his giant flukes in their direction, the little craft would be smashed into splinters.

'Get ready.'

Mr. Starbuck spoke quietly. His face was tense as he leaned against his steering oar and swore softly under his breath.

In a trice Dago Jack had shipped his oar, taken his place in the bow, and with knee braced against the forward gunwale stood ready with the long, sharp-pointed harpoon in his hands. Out of the corner of his eye David could see the iron's wooden handle. The whaleline which was attached to it lay along the thwarts between the oarsmen, wound about the loggerhead, and disappeared at last into the tub placed just in front of Mr. Starbuck. He watched that line as if hypnotized, while with a final, desperate effort he pulled on his oar.

'Let her go!'

At that moment something hissed through the air and the slack line suddenly leaped into life. The boat crashed into something dead ahead. The men were tumbled from the thwarts in a precipitate heap. A great cloud of steam burst over them and a deep roar filled the air. It was as if a cloudburst and a tidal wave had struck the little boat all at once.

For a moment it seemed certain that they had run on sure destruction. But the boat steadied a bit and was jerked about almost at right angles. As Mr. Starbuck took a quick turn about the loggerhead with the whaleline, now running out so rapidly that it smoked and sizzled as it drew tight and finally held, the boat crew found themselves being drawn through the water at the speed of an express train.

The harpoon had found its mark. The taut and quivering line held them securely fast to a mammoth whale. As he rushed off in mad, tempestuous flight, he dragged the little boat in his wake as if it were a cockle-shell.

X

ADRIFT

The Flurry

Chapter X

ADRIFT

THE whalemen called the exhilarating ride in the wake of a harpooned whale a Nantucket sleighride. Whales had been hunted from that little Massachusetts town even before New Bedford's ships took up the pursuit of Leviathan, and the Nantucket islanders had carried on their trade with an enthusiasm and daring which had given them a world-wide reputation for their courage. Always they brought back from their long voyages about Cape Horn incredible stories of the chase and exciting accounts of being dragged in their whaleboats for endless miles while fast to harpooned whales. So it was that this Nantucket name had been given to the experience to which David had long looked forward and which he was now enjoying so hugely.

Mr. Starbuck's whale tore through the water with a speed which only a frantic instinct to escape could have made possible. The little craft careened madly in its foam-streaked wake and the water rushing past rose almost as high as the gunwales. The crew were dashed with spray as they clung tensely to the thwarts. The taut line quivered and sang.

At first there had been a few minutes of wild confusion when it appeared as if the boat might be swamped any moment. The seamen, thrown completely off their balance, had had to struggle to get their oars properly shipped, and Mr. Starbuck and Dago Jack, in accordance with the custom whereby the harpooner became boatsteerer and the officer in charge went to the bow as soon as the whale was harpooned, changed their places only with the greatest difficulty. Once the whale was really off, however, the crew settled down to enjoy their thrilling ride.

How long it might last no one could say. Before Mr. Starbuck could hope to lance his fleeing prey, the boat would have to be drawn up close enough to the whale for him to reach it with his killing iron. Before that could be done, the whale would have to tire sufficiently to give the boat crew some chance of hauling in the line. And to judge by this monster's pace, it seemed full of a boundless energy.

David watched the whale ploughing through the deep with something like ecstasy. The wind blew through the boy's tousled hair and quickly dried the sweat which just a moment before had been pouring down his face. He forgot his blistered hands and sore back. He was living in the moment with complete abandon to the excitement of the chase.

'By graminy, this is something!' he kept whispering to himself. 'By graminy, this is something!'

He looked around for the other boats. Off to windward he caught sight of one of them. It too was fast to a whale, which was drawing it in a direction almost opposite to theirs. The other he could not see. Far behind them he thought he saw some dark specks bobbing up and down in the water. Could Captain Hunter's boat have met disaster? Could those specks be its crew? They were too far away to tell and there was no sign on Mr. Starbuck's part of any intention to cut the line and investigate.

And where was the Sea Turtle? They were being dragged so swiftly that he could barely make out her sails against the horizon. Soon they would be out of sight. Remembering stories of boats drawn so far from the mother ship that they were lost, it occurred to him that there was danger as well as excitement in a whale chase.

Still the whale continued in its frantic flight. It had slowed down a little from the terrific pace at which it had set out, but there was no sign of its really tiring. The wind rose; the sea was crested with whitecaps. An hour passed, and then another. Finally the sun began to go down and a dark haze spread over the water. The Sea Turtle slipped over the horizon.

The boat crew was getting restless and nervous.

'Where we goin' to, China?' muttered the oarsman next to David. 'Cripes! I wish Mr. Starbuck would cut the line. If the whale don't give us a chance to pull up soon, we're going to be lost out here. It's comin' on to blow, too.'

David shivered. It was one thing to be dragged along behind a whale while the Sea Turtle was still in sight. It was quite another to be headed out to open sea with night falling and no trace of the vessel. But Mr. Starbuck made no move. He sat morosely in the bow fingering the sharp point of his lance. He was not the man to cut loose from a whale when he was securely fast, particularly the first whale of the whole voyage. David thought, with grudging admiration for the mate's courage, that if he were in command, he was sure he would have cut long ago.

'Mr. Starbuck, sir,' one of the men at last ventured, 'it's beginnin' to blow up a bit and...'

The mate turned on him savagely.

'I'm in command here! Another word from anyone and I'll knock his block off.'

No one made any further move. In gloomy silence, the six men sat there stolidly as the boat rocked and careened in the whale's wake. For what seemed hours to David there were no signs of the animal's weakening. Mr. Starbuck would never cut loose, he thought; they would never draw up on the whale.

Unexpectedly there was a slackening of the line.

'Get a hold!' shouted the mate.

The seamen needed no order. With one accord they grabbed the whaleline and began hauling the boat in toward the now definitely tiring whale. It had at last spent its strength. It had been unable to shake out the harpoon or get free of the unusual weight it had dragged so long. Now it was idling on the surface, rising and sinking in the deep swells. Slowly the boat was pulled up. Mr. Starbuck stood in the bow with his lance in his hand.

He waited until the boat almost touched the animal's back, until the crew could hear the hot hiss of the vapor shooting from its spout-hole and feel the condensed steam pour over them in a scalding shower. Then he drew back his arm and fiercely plunged the lance deep into the whale's neck.

The monster awoke with a start, plunged madly beneath the surface, and, as its huge body swung down, the out-spreading flukes swept toward the boat.

'Stern all! Stern all, for your lives!'

The men seized their oars and began to back water frantically. It was only by a hair's breadth that the flukes cleared them. The boat was almost swamped and every man in it drenched in the flood of water which poured over the side. Then it righted itself, and as the whale broke through the surface a little in front of them, the crew again began to haul in on the line.

The maddened animal, a crimson stream flowing from the deep gash which Mr. Starbuck's lance had made in its side, was twisting and turning furiously. It was in imminent danger of their being destroyed that they approached more closely. But the whale really had little fight left. Its long run had worn it out.

As the boat drew in on one side, Mr. Starbuck for the second time hurled his lance. This time he did not let the weapon out of his hand. He slowly churned it around and around in the gaping wound. If he could pierce the great artery through which flowed the whale's blood stream, if he could find what the whalemen called its 'life,' buried somewhere there beneath the thick layer of protective blubber, the chase would be over.

At last a thick stream of blood gushed from the whale's spout-hole. The doomed animal, with a burst of frenzied energy, tried to turn upon its enemy. As the boat crew hurriedly backed off, it lashed the sea into a fury with its thrashing flukes.

'He's gone into his flurry!' shouted someone. 'We've got him now!'

David watched with amazed wonder the awesome scene of the dying whale's final struggle. Around and around the great animal swam in an ever-narrowing circle. From both the wound in its side and from its spout-hole poured the red stream of its life blood. More and more feebly it swam; more and more feebly the great flukes beat against the sea. Then with one convulsive shudder, a final upheaval of its massive body, the whale fell back helpless in the trough of the sea. At last it lay there quiet, the head strangely pointing toward the west where a faint crimson glow marked the passage of the setting sun.

'By crackity, he's dead! He's dead as a door nail.'

The men sat quietly, resting on their oars, as they watched the spectacular close to their duel with Leviathan. Here was the end of the chase. Here was victory. In the dead whale lay the symbol of their triumph over the largest of earth's creatures. Not only the country boy, witness for the first time of the death of a whale, but the entire boat crew felt curiously moved.

Mr. Starbuck quickly aroused them.

'Come on now!' he ordered brusquely. 'We got work to do yet.'

The boat was pulled over to the dead whale and a line fastened about its flukes. It had to be towed back to the Sea Turtle. Unless the ship sailed down in their direction, the whole course of the animal's flight would have to be retraced with this incredibly heavy burden dragging behind them. And the Sea Turtle was nowhere in sight. Darkness had fallen.

Still there was nothing else to do but to start back. They could not desert their prize. The men pulled doggedly, and David struggled to do his share. All the discomfort of the early stages of the chase now returned fourfold. The boy's blistered hands, his strained back, plagued him worse than ever. Without the excitement of the chase and with only the worry of what would happen if the Sea Turtle did not find them or they could not find the Sea Turtle, David was soon in an agony of pain and anxiety.

For two hours they pulled and there was no sign of the ship. It was too dark to see her unless she bore right down on them, and resting wearily on their oars, the men gazed off into space in the vain hope of a glimpse of her running lights.

It was an eerie feeling, that of being lost in the dark immensity of the ocean, alone beneath the unfriendly southern stars. But a problem of even more immediate concern confronted them. The rising sea could no longer be ignored. For some time now the wind had been whipping the water into waves which broke continually over the side of the boat. It had become necessary to bail. First with the bucket and then with their hats, the exhausted seamen tried to keep pace with the mounting water. It had become hopeless to try to pull any farther.

On Mr. Starbuck's orders they worked the boat around to the lee side of the dead whale, letting it act as a breakwater for them. This helped. They were able to bail their craft out properly. The wind continued to blow more and more stiffly, however, and not even the whale could fully protect them from the lashing fury of the waves. Then it clouded over and began to rain, pelting down on them in a heavy downpour which added still further to their discomfort and misery.

It was a full ten hours since the boat had been lowered in pursuit of the whales. Its crew had first been overheated during the long pull before the whale had been harpooned, then chilled to the bone during their mad Nantucket sleighride, and finally drenched to the skin by the sea and rain. They had had nothing to eat since breakfast, and not a man but regretted the dinner he had so scornfully thrown over the Sea Turtle's side in what now seemed such a silly revolt against poor rations. Stowed forward in the water and bread kegs were the emergency supplies every whaleboat carried, but Mr. Starbuck would not allow them to be broken out. They might need them even more later on. His blunt refusal to the request of one man that they be allowed something to eat brought home to David how grave was the peril with which they were faced.

In abject misery the boy wondered whether they could possibly survive the night, whether if they did, by some miracle of good luck, the ship would be able to find them the next day. He doubted it very much. Was this to be the end of his whaling voyage? Was this the close of his great adventure? The angry roar of the sea beat against his ears, the salt spray stung his face, the darkness shut in upon him.

Suddenly there was a shout from one of the men:

'She's sinking!'

For some mysterious reason the body of the whale had lost its buoyancy. Almost without warning it sank, and only by hastily cutting the ropes which had been thrown about its flukes to hold them in the lee was the boat saved from being dragged down with it. Then there was no protection against the sweep of wind and wave beating against the little craft with its crew of six drenched and shivering men.

The long-drawn-out nightmare of the next few hours was something which David never forgot. There was nothing they could do except keep the boat headed up into the wind and go on bailing. They all worked feverishly, Mr. Starbuck and Dago Jack as well as the oarsmen, spelling each other until exhaustion forced them to drop helplessly on the thwarts. No small craft other than a whaleboat could have outlived the night. It would have been swamped in five minutes. But a whaleboat was built to withstand whatever rough weather the sea might offer, and as long as they could keep bailing, they were all right.

Nevertheless, when at last the wind began to abate a little and the rain stopped, the boat crew had just about reached the limit of their endurance. A dull, sodden, bleary-eyed group of men apathetically watched the first glimmer of light appear in the east. If the night was over, the dawning day held out such scant hope of rescue that it was welcomed with little enthusiasm. David slumped down, too tired to care what might happen next, and fell into a dead sleep.

He did not know how long he had slept when he was awakened by a wild, excited cry:

'A sail! A sail!'

There on the horizon was a sail. The weary seamen could hardly believe their eyes. Mr. Starbuck tore off his shirt and, fastening it on the end of an oar, began to wave it frantically back and forth. The vessel was still much too far off to sight them, but no one could tell at what moment the lookout, certain to be stationed at her masthead, might pick them out. They began to row feverishly, but their only real chance of rescue was centered in the shirt fluttering bravely in the wind.

At first it was impossible to tell whether the ship was coming in their direction or not, but after a time it was evident that her course lay toward them.

'By cripes, it's the Sea Turtle!' cried one of the crew.

'No, sir,' answered another, 'that's not the Sea Turtle. But what's the difference? She's comin' our direction, ain't she? She's sure to see us.'

'I know she's the Sea Turtle. Look at the lines of her.'

'Yes, yes. By golly, you're right. It's the Sea Turtle. Hooray! Hooray!'

As the men pulled toward her, they talked and joked gaily. A vast wave of relief flooded over them. Gone were the fears and anxieties of the night, forgotten the fatigue and suffering of the past twelve hours. They were saved. The Sea Turtle was bearing directly down on them. They must already have been sighted from the masthead.

A half-hour later the six men were climbing aboard their ship's friendly deck, so thankful to feel those strong planks again beneath their feet that they completely forgot any disappointment over losing their whale.

'Well, we sure thought we'd seen the last of you,' said a friendly voice as David clambered over the rail.

David looked up as Frank gave him a hand and noted the harpooner's look of real concern.

'I thought you had, too,' he answered simply. 'Were the other boats all right?'

'We got smashed up, but no one got hurt.'

So those bobbing specks he had seen when they were first fast to their own whale had been the heads of a boat crew. Whaling was a serious business. David looked around.

'No, we ain't got a whale yet,' Frank interpreted his puzzling glance. 'We had dumfounded bad luck. We got smashed, the other boat had to cut its line, and I take it you lost your whale. Well, better luck next time. There's lots of whales in the ocean. I guess we're lucky at that, since we didn't lose any men.'

With a hearty clap on the back, the harpooner gave the boy a shove.

'Better hunt up the doctor and get some grub. We'll be lowerin' again before you know it.'

XI

TRYING–OUT

Cutting In and Boiling

Chapter XI

TRYING–OUT

ALMOST a week passed before Frank's optimistic
promise that they would soon be lowering again was
fulfilled. But this time the boats did not return empty-
handed. Captain Hunter got fast and killed his whale. A
cheerful crew turned in that night knowing that for the first
time since the Sea Turtle had started on her voyage ten
months ago, the huge carcass of a whale was securely tied
alongside the ship. It was a bull sperm whale, a sixty-
barreler according to Tim's knowing estimate, and the job
of trying-out all that oil promised plenty of work for everyone.

The next day was fortunately calm, and while the lookouts
were kept at the mastheads, everyone else except the steersman was assigned to some part of the difficult task which
for the next twenty-four hours would turn the Sea Turtle
into a combined butcher-shop and refinery. It was not
pleasant work, this business of cutting-in the whale and trying-out the oil, but the disgruntled crew of the week before
had greatly changed. They had now forgotten the causes
of their rebellion simply because they had been too busy to
think of them. With appetites whetted by long hours in

the boats, the foremast hands could not worry about how hard the ship biscuit might be or how tough the salt junk. They took life as it came and turned to their work with some enthusiasm.

The first thing to be done in the process of cutting-in the whale was to cut off its head. A platform was thrown out from the deck over the body, and the mates and boatsteerers, armed with long-handled cutting-in spades, began to hack and slice at the animal's massive neck. For the time being the rest of the crew lined the rail, watching with fascination the gluttonous activities of the sharks attracted to the carcass by the blood which was freely flowing from it.

'Look at that fellow!' David cried excitedly.

A shark larger than any of the others swam into the circle and tore viciously at a piece of half-cut blubber.

'Get him, Frank; get him!'

The harpooner looked down over the edge of the platform, his spade in his hand.

'Where's the beggar?'

'There he is! That one with the long jaw. See! He's tearing out great hunks of blubber. He'll eat the whole whale, the thief. Gosh! I'd hate to have him snapping at me.'

'I'll fix him!' exclaimed Frank. 'I'll teach him to come disturbin' us when we're workin' on a whale. There you are, you dirty beggar!'

Leaning over the platform, Frank stabbed at the shark with his spade. Just then the Sea Turtle gave a slight roll to leeward. The harpooner's spade found its mark, but Frank lost his footing on the slippery platform and only saved himself from falling entirely into the sea by catching hold of a rope with one hand. His legs were dangling over the side within a few inches of the snapping jaws of the fish below him.

'Give me a hand.'

Frank spoke quietly, but his face was an ashy gray as Mr. Macy and another man grabbed hold of him and dragged him back to his feet. It had been a narrow shave. If he had not caught hold of something, they might have been able to pull him out of the water, but not before the sharks had done their work. The harpooner knew it.

'That's what comes of not stickin' strictly to business,' he said in a gruff undertone, blaming himself and not David, whose cry had caused him to try to spear the shark. 'I'll have no more dealin's with those fish. Let 'em have all the blubber they can get.'

As the men on the platform continued their work, there was no more playing with sharks, and after a time the whale's great head was completely cut off. It was then allowed to float to the stern of the ship, where it was again tied, and the even more difficult task undertaken of peeling off the thick layer of blubber in which the body was encased. 'A regular blubber overcoat,' Tim called it.

In order to do this, ropes were swung from the masthead with heavy hooks attached to them. It was the job of the mates and harpooners to cut the blubber into slices, about fourteen inches wide, and attach the hooks in them, while the crew heaved on the windlass and peeled the blubber off in great long strips known as blanket-pieces. They came off just like the peels of an orange, the body of the whale slowly revolving in the water as the blanket-pieces were hoisted mast-high. These pieces were then lowered into the blubber room, cut off into smaller strips called horse-pieces, and the hooks lowered to peel off another section.

It was hard and dangerous work as David soon learned. He had been assigned to help guide the blanket-pieces down the hatchway into the blubber room. As they were unwound, the Sea Turtle was canted over at an angle which seemed to threaten the capsizing of the ship any moment, and if they once started swinging, anyone who got in their way would be knocked flat or smashed against the rail. Also the whole deck, and indeed every part of the ship, was now slippery with the horrid mixture of blood and oil called gurry.

David had a bad fall. As one of the blanket-pieces was cut off, the ship, relieved of the weight of the whale's body, unexpectedly righted itself and the suspended mass of blubber started to swing in his direction. At the warning shout of one of the men, he dodged quickly, but lost his footing. The next thing he knew he came up with a bang against the bulwarks, having slid all the way across the deck. He got up ruefully as the men working at the windlass jeered at his misadventure.

There was no let-up in the work of cutting-in. Mr. Starbuck was in charge and he allowed no loafing on the job. With memories of the attempted mutiny still in his mind, he kept a special eye on Dago Jack, Spider, and Heinie, the latter now fully recovered from the blow which had dropped him to the deck when he had refused the mate's order to go aft. If they showed the slightest sign of shirking, a volley of curses and once or twice a swift kick from Mr. Starbuck's restless toe brought them to their senses. As a harpooner, Dago Jack worked on the cutting-in stage, but the mate saw to it that he did his full share.

David watched these men curiously when Mr. Starbuck landed on them particularly hard. It was clear they were still discontented, looking for trouble. Whenever they were close together, the boy heard angry mutterings and oaths. But since the failure of whatever schemes they had hatched for promoting mutiny, they had lost much of their influence over the other members of the crew. The foremast hands avoided them. Thrown by themselves, Dago Jack scowled more than ever, Spider slunk about furtively, and Heinie grumbled to himself like a child who has been punished.

When, after several hours of the hardest sort of work, the last blanket-piece had been peeled off the whale's body and the stripped carcass cut loose to become the prize of the ravenous swarm of sharks, David found a chance to ask Frank what he thought of Dago Jack.

'What's he up to, do you think?' the boy inquired.

'He's just a trouble-maker, that's all,' the harpooner answered with a scornful glance at the Portuguese. 'I knew it first time I laid eyes on him. He's a bully and a coward. If he don't complain about one thing, he grumbles about another. There's one like him aboard every ship.'

'I think I've heard about him before,' David said calmly, not wanting Frank to know how queer he felt every time he thought of Dago Jack. 'My uncle used to tell about a Portuguese who was always stirring up trouble. He had a scar just like Dago Jack's. He tried to knife the mate or something.'

'Yes? Well, I wouldn't be surprised. Dago Jack's bound to make trouble every voyage. I don't know why Mr. Starbuck didn't catch on to him before, but he's got his eye on him now all right.'

'Do you think he wants to start a mutiny?'

'Oh, he just wants to make trouble. He don't know what

he's really after himself. What good would it do him if the crew mutinied? None. But he's got to be watched just the same. Has he been pickin' on you any more?'

'I'm not afraid of him,' David answered quickly. 'But he hasn't forgotten that fight we got into at the Crossed Harpoons. He's still got it in for me.'

'If he tries anything, you just let...'

Before Frank finished his sentence a thundering order from Mr. Starbuck brought them back to the work at hand. The head of the whale, still swinging from the stern, had to be bailed out. A sperm whale's best oil was found in its head. In the deep cavity called the case there might be some twenty barrels of spermaceti so pure it did not have to be boiled. It needed only to be bailed out and stowed away below. David was ordered to start this bailing.

At first, balancing himself precariously on the whale's head, he merely scooped the rich liquid out of the case by dipping in his bucket, but soon the bucket had to be lowered into the deep cavity by a rope. When at last the case was almost emptied, David himself was let down into the head to scoop up the little oil which was left at the bottom. It was a curious sticky cavern in which he found himself, with a pervasive, sweetish smell. He was glad to be pulled up into the clear ocean air when his work was at last done. Never again did he see a lamp burning whale oil or a spermaceti candle without being reminded of that brief descent into a whale's head.

With the carcass entirely disposed of, David thought that work for the day was over. It was growing late; the entire crew was weary. But Captain Hunter had no idea of calling a halt to these busy activities. No one could tell when another whale might be sighted, and there was to be no rest for those aboard the Sea Turtle until the last drop of oil had been tried-out and stowed below. Already the harpooners had started fires under the two huge iron kettles, or try-pots, in which the blubber was to be boiled.

At this stage of the process David found himself cutting up the horse-pieces of blubber into bible leaves. He had been at a loss to understand this queer name when he had first heard it, but as one of the older hands showed him what he was supposed to do, he saw what it meant. The horse-pieces had to be sliced with a mincing knife in such a way that they hung together like a book with very thin pages. So cut up, but not completely separated, they were tossed into the try-pots and allowed to boil until all the oil was separated from the fibrous matter. The sizzling liquid was then ladled out with long-handled dippers into copper containers where it was allowed to cool, and the residue, or cracklings, served as further fuel for the roaring fires in the brick ovens beneath the try-pots.

The deck of the Sea Turtle presented an outlandish spectacle. As night began to fall, the blazing fires amidships threw an unnatural glare over the group of men working about the try-works, and every so often the flames would leap into the sky, licking at the sails with darting tongues of fire. Again and again David thought the ship herself must surely catch, but no one else paid any attention to what seemed to him so grave a danger. More cracklings were thrown into the try-works by the soot-begrimed stokers, and as the hissing oil was ladled out, the boy was frantically called upon to get along faster with his bible leaves and keep the boiling kettles full.

Dense clouds of smoke hung over the vessel; the acrid smell of the burning cracklings was overpowering. Stripped

to their waists, the sweat running down their backs in greasy
rivulets, the crew worked feverishly in a bedlam of orders,
shouts, grumbles, and curses. Sometimes the whole scene
would be blurred and indistinct, then as a little oil spilled
over and the fire flared up, the figures of the men would stand
out in sharp relief.

Looking up for a moment from his busy slicing of the horse-
pieces, David wondered whether he really was aboard the
Sea Turtle or whether it was all a horrible nightmare. His
friendly companions of the forecastle appeared like so many
demons stirring some satanic brew, and Mr. Starbuck, driving them to their work with angry curses and a ready blow
for anyone who seemed to shirk, might well have been the
Devil himself.

After a time the tried-out oil was cool enough to be put in
barrels. The cooper had brought up the staves and hoops
and was hurriedly knocking them together. David was relieved of his mincing-knife and with several others of the
crew began transferring the oil into these barrels from the
copper containers. As soon as one was full, the cooper
battened down the head and it was rolled across deck to be
lowered into the hold.

This was no easy task. Although the night was fortunately
very calm and the Sea Turtle was almost stationary with her
sails backed, she rolled heavily in the swells. With decks so
slippery with gurry that it was hard to keep one's feet in any
event, maneuvering the heavy barrels was a hazardous pro-
ceeding. If they once got started across the deck, there was
no stopping them. With frantic shouts of warning, the seamen would jump out of the way and the loosed barrel would
crash into the bulwarks. Then laboriously it would have to
be rolled back again to where it could be lowered into the
hold.

One voyager aboard the Sea Turtle who had been completely mystified by these strange happenings was the little monkey, Hoppo. He was still a great friend of David's — and a wary adversary of Mr. Starbuck's — but since that day, which now seemed so long ago, when he had run off with the first mate's hat, he had not been up to any special mischief. The entire crew had become very fond of him and the only danger he ran was that of overeating. He was always being thrown scraps and always ate them.

On this night of trying-out he scampered about the deck and swung himself through the rigging in great excitement. So long as the work was about the try-pots, he did not get in anyone's way. He would approach the boiling oil cautiously, and then scamper away in perfect terror. But when the filled barrels were being trundled about the deck, Hoppo was always underfoot.

One time David was pushing hard at a barrel when he slipped and the barrel started slowly rolling back on him.

'Look out!' shouted one of the crew. 'It's coming down on you!'

David jumped aside.

'The monkey! The monkey!'

'Look at Hoppo!'

There was a chorus of shouts and David saw that Hoppo, somehow entangled in a line, was right in the path of the barrel and apparently unable to extricate himself from his perilous position.

'Pull him out of the way!'

'Grab that line!'

'Get hold of the barrel! Swing it around!'

There was a rush to Hoppo's rescue. Sliding about on the oily deck, every man near enough to be of help tried to do something. David made a dive toward the rope in which the monkey was caught, Frank almost knocked Dago Jack off his feet as he rushed across the deck, and three seamen threw themselves against the now fast-rolling barrel to divert its course. Everything else was forgotten. One of the men dipping out the oil dropped his dipper. The fire blazed up so fiercely that the whole deck was lit up by the leaping flames.

With a quick jerk David pulled at the line he had hastily grabbed, the heavy barrel thundered past to hit the bulwark with a resounding crash, and Hoppo was safe. Freeing himself from the tangle of ropes, the monkey scampered away. Chattering noisily, he made straight for a safe spot within the galley and was not seen again that night.

'Get back to work. No more tomfoolery.'

Captain Hunter himself had seen the rescue from the quarterdeck. But he had not given his order until he, too, was satisfied that Hoppo was safe. Mr. Starbuck said nothing.

The trying-out was almost over at the time of this incident. It was not long before the fires were allowed to die down and the last of the oil lay cooling. Mr. Starbuck's watch was sent below and the watch on deck left to stow the rest of the oil as soon as it could be handled. There would be plenty of work tomorrow cleaning up, but that night the worn-out seamen threw themselves into their bunks just as they were.

David had hardly rolled in before he was fast asleep.

XII

A CALL AT JAPAN

The Wreck

Chapter XII

A CALL AT JAPAN

DO YOU think we'll get whales on the Japan grounds?'
'Why, sonny, there're so many sperm playin' around
that part of the ocean they keep bumpin' into each other.
Yes, sir, it's crowded with 'em. It's grand sport fishin' there,
I tell you.'

It was almost a month since the Sea Turtle had tried out
her first whale. Three more had been taken in quick succession after that successful lowering, and then for a week not
a single spout had been sighted. Captain Hunter had decided
to head north toward the Japan grounds and the whaleship
was now nearing them. David had sought out Tim, as usual
busy sharpening up the irons, to find out what he could of the
chances of good luck in this new field of operations.

'Did you ever land in Japan?' he asked the old sailor.

'Land in Japan? Crackity, you can't land there. Nobody's ever got ashore in Japan. Why, those Japanners
would kill you off quick as a flash. I've heard tell they're
cannibals, too. Leastways they eat raw fish, and if you eat
raw fish, I guess you'll eat anything. No, sir, those Japanners
may be little fellows, but you want to keep away from 'em
all the same.'

More than that David could not discover about this mysterious country. To every other question he asked, Tim shook his head gloomily and muttered something about 'those little Japanners eatin' raw fish.' It only served to arouse the boy's curiosity. He wished he would get a chance to see some of them and to land on their forbidden shores. He wondered what they were really like.

Several days later the lookout sighted a strange object floating in the sea. It seemed to be the wreck of some sort of craft, but it was neither a whaleship nor a whaleboat. It was too small for the one, and too large for the other. As the Sea Turtle bore down on it, there were many wild guesses as to what it might be.

'By gar, I know what she is!' finally exclaimed one of the foremast hands who had been on the Japan grounds before. 'I'll bet five plugs of tobacco she's one of them Japanner junks. She got wrecked somehow, and here she is.'

'I wonder if anybody's still aboard her?' David asked.

As if in answer to his question, he caught sight of a piece of blue cloth fluttering from one of the derelict's broken masts.

'There's a signal! There's a signal!' he cried excitedly. 'There's somebody on board.'

Captain Hunter ordered a boat lowered, and as the Sea Turtle drifted lazily in the slight breeze, the crew lined the rails to watch their boat pulling toward the wreck. They saw it draw alongside, apparently take several men aboard, and then start back toward the ship. When it was close enough, they could see five woe-begone and bedraggled figures huddled in the bow, apparently so exhausted that they could not stand on their feet.

They were 'Japanners' all right. Their small size, the yellow texture of their skin, their dark oval eyes, were unmistakable evidence of their race. One or two of them wore rough cloth shirts; the rest had on nothing except a sort of breechcloth. As the seamen looked down on them, they gazed back apathetically with blank, unseeing eyes. One of them was moaning quietly.

Captain Hunter came over to the rail.

'Haul 'em up on deck,' he ordered gruffly. 'Give 'em some rum and water and a pair of pants apiece. Then what we'll do with the beggars, the Lord only knows. Hurry up with it. We ain't goin' to spend all day rescuin' a lot of half-drowned Japanners.'

He turned away and stalked back to the quarterdeck.

'Why not take 'em home, sir?' asked Mr. Macy.

'They won't let you land in their fool country,' Captain Hunter answered sharply.

'I know that, sir. But we've saved these fellows' lives. If we take 'em into Yeddo harbor, they'll have to treat us decently. They might even let us go ashore. We've got supplies aboard ship which might make some sort of trade. I've heard there's lots of gold in Japan. It might be worth the chance, sir.'

'Maybe you're right at that,' Captain Hunter answered after a minute's thought. 'It wouldn't do any harm to try. We'll take a look at the chart.'

David had heard most of this conversation and, as the two officers went into the Captain's cabin, he rushed forward with his news. Most of the crew had gathered in the fore-castle where the boy found them doing their best to persuade the dazed Japanese sailors to take their grog. They seemed to have no idea of what was expected of them and weakly resisted every attempt to make them drink the fiery liquid. But the friendly seamen would not let them off. The rum was poured down their throats by main force.

'We're going to Japan!' shouted David, as he half fell down the ladder into the forecastle. 'We're going to Japan!'

His announcement created the sensation he had hoped. No one aboard the Sea Turtle had ever seen the country, but innumerable tales about it had floated from one forecastle to another ever since whaling had first been tried in the Japan Sea. No member of the crew but thought he would somehow win great riches if they visited Yeddo. The Japanese sailors were treated with more care than ever and stowed away comfortably in bunks. Heinie solicitously put his blanket over one of them.

A few days later it became known that the Sea Turtle was off the Japanese coast and never was the first sight of land awaited more eagerly. To the surprise of some of the green hands, it looked no different from any other land when at last it came in view. Japan apparently had rocks and trees and mountains much as other parts of the world. Nevertheless, as the ship rounded a point of land and sailed slowly up a wide channel, opening into a broad harbor, an impressive spectacle greeted the Sea Turtle's crew.

The harbor itself was filled with shipping. There were scores of vessels of all sizes: great seagoing junks, with three and four masts, on whose bows were painted fearsome devils' eyes; fishing vessels with colored sails of woven matting; smaller craft, sculled by a single oar, which darted quickly in and out among the other ships. The shore line was heavily wooded, and at the far end of the harbor was a cluster of houses, tiny houses with gently sloping roofs.

But what dominated the scene was the majestic beauty of a great mountain whose cone-shaped peak rose high above the clouds massed against its smooth slopes. It seemed to float there in the sky. David had never seen a lovelier sight.

As the Sea Turtle came in and dropped anchor, it was clear that her arrival caused general consternation. She was at first given a wide berth by the rest of the shipping, but soon a number of small boats approached and, their number swiftly increasing, they gradually formed a ring about the whaleship. It was then seen that lines were being passed from one to another of these boats until a great circle of the little craft, all tied together, completely surrounded the Sea Turtle. Beyond them another ring was formed, and then a third. There were hundreds of the boats, each manned by four or five Japanese. The crews of those in the inner circle were armed with long lances. The Sea Turtle was a prisoner.

It was late in the day when the whaleship anchored and darkness had fallen before the three circles of surrounding boats were all in position. No one of the craft came within hailing distance; Captain Hunter did not consider it advisable to lower one of his own boats. That night the crew turned in with some nervousness as to what the morning might bring forth.

They did not have long to wait. Soon after daybreak a boat approached the Sea Turtle. It was much like the others, but an imposing awning was spread over its stern. Its crew was armed with lances and short swords, and beneath the awning, sitting cross-legged, were four dignified Japanese in long silk gowns, their hair drawn up into topknots. From the sash of the gown of each man protruded two sword handles.

The boat drew alongside the Sea Turtle. With a serious and important air its passengers, evidently high officials, climbed aboard the whaleship and walked slowly toward the quarterdeck.

Captain Hunter, followed by Mr. Starbuck and Mr. Macy, came out to meet them.

They bowed very politely and without a word handed
Captain Hunter a long document written in Japanese
characters.

'What's all this?' he demanded bluntly.

One of the officials bowed again, then quietly pointed to
the document and said something in his own language.

'I haven't any idea what you're sayin',' broke in Captain
Hunter. 'Mr. Macy, you got us into this. What's he talkin'
about, that fellow in the blue dress? What's all this funny
writin' mean?'

Mr. Macy could understand no more than Captain
Hunter. He tried by gestures to explain the Sea Turtle's
mission, but it was obviously impossible to make any
headway.

Watching the scene from the ship's waist, David's eye
wandered from the Captain in his baggy trousers and dirty
reefer to the neatly gowned Japanese officials. His rough
appearance, with a two days' growth of beard and grimy
finger nails, his violent manner, stood in marked contrast to
the almost dainty dress and perfect composure of the Japanese. He knew with what intolerant scorn Captain Hunter re-
garded the queerly dressed heathen; he had somewhat the
same feelings himself; but for a moment he wondered what
the Japanese must think of Captain Hunter and his scare-
crow crew. But there was no clue to their feelings in the
polite mask which guarded their thoughts.

'Bring up those fellows we rescued,' Captain Hunter at
last ordered in desperation.

The five Japanese sailors were brought on deck, but the
moment they saw their fellow countrymen they seemed
transfixed with fear. They threw themselves precipitately
on their knees, knocking their heads on the deck, and began
to talk rapidly and all together.

The officials had given some indication of surprise at their appearance, but paid little attention to whatever it might be they were saying. Drawing back their gowns, they looked down at them haughtily. Finally the spokesman of the officials gave a brief, curt order. Almost before the words were out of his mouth, the five men had scrambled to their feet, rushed to the rail, and dropped into the waiting boat.

'That's gratitude for you,' muttered Captain Hunter, watching these developments with amazement. 'Now what about these fellows?'

The four officials were again bowing low. Two of them returned to their boat; two remained aboard the Sea Turtle. What they planned to do, it was impossible to tell. The two who remained aboard the ship stood quietly by the mainmast, alert and attentive, and made no further attempt to communicate with either officers or crew.

In a short time, however, another boat was seen approaching the whaleship. It drew alongside, and its crew, like so many monkeys, climbed up the side and began to unload on the Sea Turtle's deck a great quantity of casks, boxes, crates.

'What's all this?' demanded Captain Hunter, appearing from his cabin.

One of the Japanese officials stepped forward and bowed deeply, then gracefully spreading out his hands, he made a gesture which clearly indicated that the heaped-up articles represented a gift for the officers and crew of the whaleship. There were great casks of water, boxes of rice, crates of fresh vegetables, and, carefully packed away, several sets of delicate chinaware, lacquer bowls, and lovely painted vases.

The boxes were opened up and the wondering crew crowded
about to look over their contents with keen curiosity. There
was a low mumbling of admiring comments:

'By gosh, here's some decent grub at last!'

'Look at them little cups, would yer!'

'What do you hold the dern things by? They ain't got no
handles.'

'Gee, what a pretty picture!'

In the meantime the Japanese official took out from beneath the voluminous folds of his gown another long scroll.
The characters on this document were of gigantic size, looking for all the world like the footprints of a chicken. The
Japanese bowed lower than ever. Then, pointing to the sky,
he fell to his knees, and, without raising his eyes from the
deck, held the strange document out to Captain Hunter.

'For land's sake,' that mystified whaler exclaimed, 'this
thing must be from their Emperor or somebody. We better
be careful of it. What are the jackanapes goin' to do next?
Tell 'em we're much obliged, Mr. Macy, and that now we're
ready to go ashore and look things over for ourselves. Make
'em understand somehow.'

For a moment Captain Hunter watched his mate's futile
efforts to tell the Japanese they wanted to land, and then
turned away impatiently.

'Lower a boat there,' he ordered.

Several seamen jumped to obey, but no sooner had they
put their hands on the falls of one of the whaleboats than the
Japanese aboard the vessel drew their swords and advanced
menacingly on them. The seamen hesitated.

'Let's throw the little fellow overboard!' shouted Frank,
moving over toward one of the officials. He towered over
him by a good foot and in his unwieldy strength was quite

capable of picking up the slight Japanese and tossing him anywhere he chose. But the official did not move an inch, did not flicker an eyebrow. He kept his sword firmly grasped in long, delicate fingers.

There was a confused murmur from the Sea Turtle's crew. Some of them were for backing up Frank in a rush on the Japanese; others held back and edged toward the rack of whaling irons.

'Don't touch 'em!' ordered Captain Hunter. 'Stand back, all of you!'

He looked curiously at the Japanese officials with their drawn swords, glanced over the side toward the ring of boats which surrounded the Sea Turtle, and then again looked at the officials. Taking off his battered sea cap, he scratched his head.

'Gosh almighty!' he exclaimed. 'What the devil's to do now, Mr. Macy?'

'I don't know, sir. We could get out our pistols and shoot up a few of these fellows. I guess we could match any number of 'em with whaling irons. But where that would get us, I don't know. Why, there're hundreds of those little boats surrounding us and half a dozen armed men on each of 'em. They don't seem to want us to go ashore, and I guess if they don't want us to, there ain't much we can do about it.'

The Japanese were quietly watching Captain Hunter and Mr. Macy. When it appeared that they understood they weren't going to be allowed to lower a boat, the official who had brought the scroll pointed out to sea and made a gesture which evidently meant to suggest that the Sea Turtle get under way.

'Maybe we can't land, but they can't get rid of us as

quickly as all that,' Captain Hunter muttered. 'Can't they see which way the wind's blowin'?''

He held up his hand and tried to explain that with a strong breeze sweeping up the channel, his ship had to wait a change in weather. The Japanese ignored him. At a sharp order one of the men in the boat began to wave a flag, and immediately there was a great commotion among the boats encircling the whaleship. The lines which tied them together were cast off and their crews started sculling rapidly into a new formation. With amazing speed they lined the boats up four abreast in a long row leading out of the harbor. Then the lines were brought out again and each boat was tied to the one preceding it, while from the four nearest the Sea Turtle heavy hawsers were taken aboard the whaleship.

As if hypnotized and without any order from the quarter-deck, four of the whaleship's crew carried these hawsers forward and made them fast. They then looked expectantly toward Captain Hunter.

'Well, I'm hornswoggled! If this don't beat the Dutch!'

There was no doubt of what the Japanese intended. They were going to tow the Sea Turtle out of the harbor. In the teeth of the wind they planned to tow the ship down the channel by the combined strength of several hundred of their little boats, even though they were equipped with nothing more than a single sculling oar apiece. Captain Hunter waved his hand helplessly and gave the order to raise the anchor.

The Sea Turtle moved slowly as the Japanese oarsmen, at a signal from the whaleship's deck, dug in vigorously with their long sweeps. For a while it appeared impossible that they could get her under way. The wind and waves seemed to conspire to hold her back. But the flotilla of little boats gradually got their tow started and at a snail's pace the strange procession moved down the channel toward the open sea.

Captain Hunter paced his quarterdeck nervously.

'I never thought to see the like of this,' he kept saying to himself. 'I never thought to see the like of this. Towed out to sea by a fleet of Japanners! By the great horn spoon! The Sea Turtle towed by a fleet of Japanners!'

The crew lined the rail. Standing alone by the mainmast were the two Japanese officials who had stayed aboard the ship. With calm, impassive eyes they watched the progress of the long train of little boats.

For a full twenty miles the Sea Turtle was towed. Then at another signal the Japanese craft cast off their ropes. One of them drew alongside the whaleship. With courteous bows to Captain Hunter the two officials went over the side, and in a few minutes the whole fleet of boats was being sculled back toward the harbor.

The order to raise sail was given from the quarterdeck and soon the Sea Turtle was beating her way out to sea under her own power. The Japanese shore, the towering peak of the mountain which overlooked the harbor, slowly faded from sight.

XIII

AN UNEXPECTED LOWERING

The Boats are Lowered

Chapter XIII

AN UNEXPECTED LOWERING

THE Sea Turtle crowded on all sail as soon as she was well off the coast of Japan. Captain Hunter now regretted the foolish impulse which had led him to visit that inhospitable country, and was anxious to get back on the grounds where they might expect to raise whales. It was late in the season. Too little oil had been obtained so far on the voyage for him to feel very happy about the time he had wasted over the shipwrecked Japanese sailors.

A few days later they were slowly cruising back and forth over the small area in which experience had proved that sperm whales were most likely to be found at this time of the year. Five other sails were in sight, and as they drew near one of these vessels a boat was seen being lowered. Aboard the Sea Turtle the watch on deck carefully scanned the horizon for any sign of whales which might have been noticed from the other whaleship.

'Do you see anythin'?' Captain Hunter shouted at the man at the Sea Turtle's masthead.

'Nary a spout,' came back the lookout's call.

'Humph! I suppose he wants to gam,' Captain Hunter said gloomily to Mr. Starbuck. 'We ain't got no time for it.

It's all right to have a gam when you're full of oil, but the Sea Turtle hasn't really started yet.'

David was having his trick at the wheel, and overhearing Captain Hunter's remark, wondered what on earth he meant by 'gam.' Then he remembered hearing the term before. It meant visiting, an exchange of boat crews between two whaleships meeting at sea. He waited eagerly for the next command and was greatly excited when Captain Hunter, seeing that the boat from the unknown vessel was really headed toward the Sea Turtle, ordered the sails backed. Another moment and the strangers were within hailing distance.

'Sea Turtle ahoy,' shouted a burly figure seated in the boat's stern. 'I'm Captain Falks of the Globe, eight months out of Nantucket. Can I come aboard for a gam?'

'Certainly. Glad to see you, Captain Falks,' called back Captain Hunter with forced joviality. 'Have you had any luck hereabouts?'

'Not yet. Whales are scarce as hens' teeth. We ain't lowered in more'n a week.'

'Well, I suppose I might as well let a boat go over to the Globe then. Come on aboard, Captain. I'll...Mr. Macy, if you want to gam, take a crew and pull over to the Globe. But mind you, don't forget what we're here for. If any whales are sighted, be ready for 'em. We might have a race for it with the Globe's boats.'

'All right, sir,' answered the second mate. 'I'd like a gam, but I'd like it a lot better to lower in real earnest.'

To David's great joy he was ordered into Mr. Macy's boat, as was also Frank, and in high spirits they were soon pulling over to the Globe. Her crew welcomed them on deck boisterously, and while Mr. Macy went to the quarterdeck to join the Globe's officers, the seamen gathered in the waist. A round of grog was just being handed out when David was summoned aft.

'Mr. Foley here has some news for you,' Mr. Macy said when the boy reached the quarterdeck.

'News for me, sir?'

'Well, I don't know as you'd just exactly called it news,' answered Mr. Foley, who was apparently first mate of the Globe. 'Captain Bob Worth's your uncle, eh?'

For a moment David was too startled to answer.

'Yes, sir,' he finally gulped. 'Have you heard anything...'

'Not so fast, lad,' Mr. Foley interrupted in a kindly tone. 'I don't know what's happened to your uncle, but we shipped a hand at Honolulu about a year ago who'd been aboard the Rover. He said she'd gone down somewhere near the Fijis.'

'And Uncle Bob?'

'That's what was funny about his story. First he said he'd been saved. Then he said he'd been lost with his ship. He acted mighty funny about it, this fellow. He was sort of mysterious.'

'What did he mean?'

'I don't know. There was once talk about mutiny aboard that ship, but nothin' seemed to jibe in this fellow's yarn. It had me guessin' at the time.'

David would have liked to ask the Globe's mate more, but it was clear he really knew nothing of the Rover's fate except this vague tale of shipwreck, which gave no real clue as to whether Uncle Bob had survived or not. But somehow it all awoke the boy's hopes, and he became more convinced than ever that his uncle was either marooned on a desert island or held captive by natives. He left the quarterdeck very thoughtfully on Mr. Macy's motion of dismissal.

'Well, mates,' he heard one of the Globe's crew, a jovial-looking fellow in blue dungarees say as he drew near, 'we got a pretty good fiddler aboard ship. What would you say to a couple of jigs or a bit of clog dancin', seein' as how you're visitors and ought to have some entertainment?'

'A little skylarkin' would suit us better, mate,' answered Frank. 'How about a rough-and-tumble wrestlin' bout? There're five of us; we'll take on any five of you.'

'You're on!' exclaimed the Globe's spokesman eagerly. 'That's a sight better than dancin' any day in the week.'

While the rest of the seamen gathered in a circle about them, the Sea Turtle's boat crew and five of the Globe's crew prepared for their bout. Catch-as-catch-can, all holds allowed, was the order of the day, and amid the noisy cheers and jeers of the onlookers, the ten seamen were soon rolling about the deck in a mad tangle of arms and legs.

David forgot for the time the story about the Globe. His opponent was a boy only slightly older than himself, although a good deal heavier, and before he quite realized what was happening to him, he found himself flat on the deck with his arms pinioned to his sides. With a quick roll, he threw the other boy off and tried to get a hold on him which would keep him down. But he couldn't do it. His opponent squirmed out of his grip and soon was on top of David again. They were an evenly matched pair. It was the best scrap of the whole affair. The delighted sailors cheered them on enthusiastically, first encouraging one, then the other.

Together they rolled halfway across the deck, and then

David thought he saw his chance. He gave a sharp twist, broke the other's hold, got a strong grip on his shoulders, and pressed him slowly down. They were both panting furiously, both tiring. David summoned all his energy, pressed down...

'She blows! She blows! And sparm at that!'

Instinctively David relaxed his grip and sprang to his feet. So did the other wrestlers. There was a wild rush for the rail. The distant spout of a whale...

'Man the boats!'

The Globe's crew ran to the davits; the five seamen from the Sea Turtle needed no order. They were over the bulwarks in an instant, piling pell-mell into their boat which lay gently bumping against the Globe's side.

'Cast off!' shouted Mr. Macy as he jumped in after them and grabbed his steering oar.

But a line had been taken aboard the Globe, and in their hurry no one had thought to throw it off. Mr. Macy whipped out his knife and cut it.

'Now, pull for it, lads!' he called. 'Burn me, if we don't show our heels to the Globe. We'll teach those sons-of-sea-cooks how to catch whales. Pull as you never pulled before. There's plum duff and grog for every man of you if we get fast first, but I'm darned if I won't have you keel-hauled if anyone gets in ahead of us. Pull, lads, pull!'

Neither David nor any one else in the crew had stopped long enough to see where the whale was, and now with their backs in the direction they were going, they had no idea of what was happening. But they could see that two boats from the Globe had been lowered and were just behind them. It was going to be a race, and a close one.

'You see those boats behind us?' shouted the mate, glancing quickly over his shoulder. 'They're both going to stay behind us. We can beat 'em with our hands tied. But don't tie your hands, you good-for-nothing scoundrels! Pull, I tell you, pull! There she blows! She blows! Oh, she's a beaut! A sixty-barreler, if I ever saw one. She's a darling! Pull! Pull!'

'They've lowered from the Sea Turtle!' he added excitedly. 'There're our two boats and the Globe's. But we can beat 'em all! We can beat 'em all! Put your backs into it, lads, put your backs into it!'

David was pulling even harder than he had at the first lowering. He could see the boats from the Globe and out of the corner of his eye caught a glimpse of those from the Sea Turtle. Six boats and one whale! They had to get fast. His breath came in quick, short gasps; his entire body was bathed in sweat; every muscle ached. He gritted his teeth and pulled still harder.

They were tearing through the water, but the other boats kept pace with them. Then, as Mr. Macy shifted the course a little, swearing softly under his breath, the two from the Globe crept up on them. David still had no idea of how far off the whale might be, but it was going to be a neck-and-neck race.

'Hold your oars!'

The order came unexpectedly.

David looked around. There was nothing in sight. The whale must have sounded. In the other boats the order to hold their oars had also been given, and in tense impatience their crews waited for the whale to come to the surface. The six boats were closely bunched. It was anybody's whale, and the first to get a harpoon in him would have the prize. That was the unwritten law of the whaling grounds. Panting for breath and eyeing the other boats anxiously, Mr. Macy's crew rested on their oars.

'Pull!'

With a sweep of his steering oar Mr. Macy swung the boat around and they were off again, just a fraction of a second before the whale was sighted from the other boats.

For a time they kept so near together that no one of the boats could really be said to be in the lead. Gradually Mr. Macy's and one from the Globe drew ahead. But these two were so evenly matched that neither could outdistance the other. First one would get a few feet ahead, then the other.

Mr. Macy was alternately cursing and encouraging his straining crew.

'You dodgasted idiots! Are you going to let those land-lubbers beat us? Call yourselves whalemen? Cripes! I never saw such sojerin'! Are you asleep there, you flat-faced son of a Maltese goat? Oh, lads! Put me next to this lovely whale! I'll give you all my tobacco. We can show 'em our heels if you'll only put your hearts into it. That's more like it. That's pullin' for you. We're gettin' somewhere now. Hooray! We'll show 'em! Together, now, lads, pull as if your lives depended on it.'

Very slowly the boat forged a little ahead. But only for a few minutes could it keep its lead. Again the Globe's boat drew up. Its crew was pulling as desperately as were David and his companions. Never had two whaleboats set such a terrific pace. The water flew past.

There was a movement in the other boat and the harpooner shipped his oar. At the same moment Mr. Macy ordered Frank to get ready. They were close on the whale now. David could hear it, smell it. The boat rocked in its churned-up wake.

Then, with a bitter groan, Mr. Macy unexpectedly threw his weight against the steering oar; the boat swung abruptly to port. David could see nothing, but he realized that the whale must have shifted its course. It gave a distinct advantage to the other boat. It was now a little ahead of them, nearer the whale. So close were they both to the onrushing animal, that the Globe's boat blocked any apparent chance for them to get fast.

But just as the other harpooner drew back his arm ready to dart his iron, there was a sudden hissing noise. Something flew through the air, and sank with a quivering thud deep into the whale's side. Frank had pitchpoled, thrown his iron over the other boat. The dangling line from his harpoon almost caught his rival in a flying loop. Instinctively dodging it, the Globe's harpooner lost his balance in the very act of throwing his own iron and missed his aim entirely.

With a sudden jerk David's boat keeled half over, narrowly missing a crash against the side of the Globe's boat. The line drew taut, the boat righted itself and they were off. By as expert a feat of harpooning as any whaleman could perform, Frank had got fast even though the other boat was actually nearer the whale when he threw his own iron.

As they shot past the Globe's boat in a mad whirl of angry water, a gleeful crew shouted back happy insults at their disappointed rivals.

'Hope I didn't make you lose yer balance!' called the triumphant Frank. 'You'll excuse me fer not noticin' yer was there.'

'Guess you got all tired wrestling!' was David's joyous contribution. 'You'd better rest up before you lower another time.'

There was no reply from the other boat, now rapidly dropping astern. Its crew were somewhat dazed by the startling way in which their prize had been stolen right out of their hands. The Globe's harpooner was gloomily pulling in his line, shaking his head as if he still could not quite realize what had happened.

For almost two hours Mr. Macy's boat was dragged by the harpooned whale. Somewhat apprehensively, David began to wonder if they were going to have the same experience as he had had on the previous whale chase. He wondered if Mr. Macy would refuse to cut the line as stubbornly as had Mr. Starbuck. He rather feared he would. Consequently, when the whale began to slacken its pace while the Sea Turtle was still in sight, the boy felt more relieved than he liked to admit.

'All right, lads, pull up on him,' came Mr. Macy's quiet command.

The crew seized the whaleline and began drawing it in vigorously. The whale made no move; it seemed exhausted by its long flight. But just when they were almost on it and the second mate was ready to throw his lance, the great animal sounded. With an immense heave it threw its flukes into the air and dove straight down. The line was jerked out of the men's hands and began to run out so fast that it fairly sizzled.

'Let go the line! Let go the line!' Mr. Macy shouted. 'Cripes! I was just about to lance the dodgasted crittur.'

They sat helplessly by while the line continued to run out, fathom after fathom. The whale seemed bound for the very bottom of the ocean. It did not look as if it would ever end its deep dive. The whole length of line disappeared and a second line had to be warped onto it. But still the whale pulled it after him until only a few rapidly disappearing coils were left in even the second tub.

They couldn't afford to lose this whale, and waited nervously to see what was going to happen. The line, now made fast, gradually grew taut. The weight of the whale tugged at the boat; dragged down the bow. Mr. Macy took out his knife. Another minute and he'd have to cut. That strong downward pull would swamp them, draw the boat down in the whale's descending wake. With a gloomy scowl Mr. Macy held the edge of his blade to the rope. The boat swung around as a sea broke over its prow; the crew were ready to jump.

'Here goes...'

But Mr. Macy had barely opened his mouth before the line slackened. He jerked his knife away. The boat suddenly righted itself as the pressure relaxed, almost throwing overboard the men poised on the gunwales.

'Hooray!' shouted David. 'We'll get him now!'

Again they started pulling in on the line. It came up easily and endless fathoms were coiled in the two tubs. After a time they knew why. The whale came to the surface and broke water not far off with a terrific splash. There it lay quietly, sending up in quick succession brief spouts of watery vapor.

The boat approached warily. This time the hunted animal gave no sign of either running or sounding. Mr. Macy seized his lance firmly and stood ready to throw.

'Now!' he muttered to himself.

The sharp weapon flew through the air and sank deep into the whale. Mr. Macy pulled on the line and drew out the lance, ready to plunge it again into the now badly wounded animal. Curiously it made no move. Even when the iron pierced its side a second time, there was only a quiver of its giant frame. Mr. Macy ordered the crew to bring him in closer.

'He's spouting blood! He's spouting blood!' cried one of the crew.

'By gum, he is!' exclaimed the second mate. 'He's done for already. I'll be blowed. That deep-sea dive must have been too much for him. He just wore himself out. Stern all, lads. We'll give him a clear berth and see what happens.'

They backed water well out of reach of the whale's flukes as the blood shot out of its spout-hole in convulsive jets and trickled from the wound in its side. But the animal lay like a dead weight on the surface of the sea. Finally it seemed to shudder all over and the men could almost imagine they heard a dying groan. Then even its feeble spouting stopped. No doubt of it; the whale was dead.

It did not take long to get a line about its flukes and start towing the body back to the ship. And it was a short pull. The Sea Turtle was bearing down in their direction and in less than an hour ship and boat were alongside each other.

'Captain Hunter, sir,' called Mr. Macy as soon as they were in hailing distance, 'we got your whale for you! He's a beaut, too! Sixty barrels as sure as I live.'

'A good job, Mr. Macy, a good job!' Captain Hunter called back in a hearty tone. 'I'm sure glad the Globe didn't beat us to it. I saw that bit of pitchpolin'. Cripes, though, I'd like to've seen Captain Falks's face when that harpoon sailed over his boat!'

XIV

THE FIJI ISLANDS

Scrimshaw

Chapter XIV

THE FIJI ISLANDS

FRANK'S spectacular harpooning started a run of good luck for the Sea Turtle. She stayed on the Japan grounds two weeks and captured eighteen whales. It was a period of work such as the crew had not had since their first days at sea, but the hold was now beginning to fill slowly with heavy casks of oil and the men were cheerful with the prospect of a profitable voyage.

But luck changes quickly in hunting for whales, as in angling for smaller fish, and, after these two strenuous weeks, a period of such dogged ill-fortune set in that again and again the foremast hands would have welcomed not only the excitement of lowering, but even the grueling labor of trying-out.

It was borne in on David that a whaling voyage was altogether different from what he had imagined it to be. There was all the excitement he had foreseen. He could never forget the storm about Cape Horn, his first lowering or the visit to Japan, but these incidents were high lights in many months of quiet and eventless cruising when nothing at all happened to break the day-by-day monotony of the voyage. It was now some eighteen months since the Sea Turtle had sailed from New Bedford. As the ship cruised slowly south, carefully combing the waters of the Great South Sea for any sign of whales, the dull routine of their life began to fray the tempers of the crew as it had during that previous period of prolonged inactivity which had almost ended in mutiny.

David had his own reasons for impatience. He could not forget what he had heard aboard the Globe. When he had started on the voyage he had had a boyish idea that somehow or other he would find out what had happened to Uncle Bob. As the voyage progressed, he had about given up all hope. Now the idea had been born again. He was anxious to get farther south, to meet other ships which might have further information on the fate of the Rover's crew, to visit the islands where perhaps there might be some clue to his uncle's whereabouts should he be still alive. There was nothing he could do to further his quest, but in the long hours of his watch on deck, he often imagined finding his uncle and rescuing him by some heroic deed.

There was so little to be done aboard ship in the calm, languorous days of the southern cruise that he tried every possible method of killing time. He carefully and methodically patched all his clothes, now ragged and worn by rough sea usage; read over the half-dozen books he had brought with him again and again, and spent long hours playing checkers with Frank. He kept pretty much aloof from the bickering and quarreling which was again an everyday occurrence in the forecastle, and avoided the still trouble-making trio of Dago Jack, Spider, and Heinie just as much as he possibly could.

One day he came across Tim carving away busily with his jackknife at one of the prettiest pieces of scrimshaw work he had ever seen. It was fascinating to watch the rough, gnarled hands of the blacksmith skillfully cutting the hard piece of whalebone.

'What are you making, Tim?' he asked.

'This here's a jaggin' wheel,' replied the old man.

'A jagging wheel?'

'Yes, sir, a jaggin' wheel. Your ma would know what it is, even if you don't. Ain't you ever seen one? You see it has a little wheel on the end here; you run it over the pie crust to give it a scalloped edge, and you can't make a good scalloped edge without a whalebone jaggin' wheel. I'm surprised you don't know that, David.'

'Could you teach me how to do it?'

'There's nothin' to teach. It's just practice. I've made hundreds of the dern things. You got to have a lot of time, that's all. You can't do scrimshawin' in a hurry. But on a voyage like this, you get time to make almost anythin'. I carved a little whaleship one voyage which was a beaut.'

David decided to try scrimshawing. He put a good edge on his knife and started on a piece of bone Tim gave him. He thought he'd make a whaleboat. The blacksmith grinned, but said nothing. For two days the boy worked, whittling away every spare moment he got. At the end of that time the piece of bone looked as much like a whale as a whaleboat. He didn't seem to be able to make any progress at all.

He decided he was working too slowly and began slicing away with all his strength at the brittle bone. Of course it cracked.

'Oh, shucks!' he exclaimed. 'I guess I'm not much good at this scrimshawing. How can you be so patient, Tim? You been working on that piece of bone a week and you're not finished carving the handle even.'

Tim looked up.

'I guess I'm a little older'n you. I'm not in such a gol-danged hurry. I was afraid when you started that whaleboat, you'd get fidgety before you were through. Try somethin' easier.'

'No, I guess it's too slow for me. What I want is to lower and get a chance to harpoon a whale myself. That's what I want.'

'Don't get jumpity, lad,' Tim said kindly. 'You'll get your chance yet.'

With scrimshawing out, David tried to think of something else to do. He decided to keep a log of just what happened aboard ship. This didn't help very much, and at the end of the week he looked it over mournfully:

Sunday: set sails; scrubbed decks. Most of crew spent morning patching clothes, scrimshawing or playing checkers. Heinie in quarrel over card game. Beef and rice for dinner. Nothing in afternoon. Wind moderate.

Monday: set sails; scrubbed decks. Crew mending spare sails. Fish and beans for dinner. Lookout thought he saw spout but mistaken. Calm.

Tuesday: set sails; scrubbed decks. Boats lowered after por-poises; didn't get any. Pork and beans for dinner. Mr. Starbuck told Spider he'd flog him if he didn't stop grumbling. Most of crew playing cards in forecastle. Moderate wind.

Wednesday: set sails; scrubbed decks. No whales sighted; nothing. Beef and dried peas for dinner. Hoppo fell in coffee bucket and upset it. Mr. Starbuck pretty mean with some of green hands. Moderate wind.

Thursday: set sails; scrubbed decks. Heinie fell asleep at crow's nest. Put on bread and water. More grumbling. Pork and beans for dinner. Afternoon, nothing. Calm.

Friday: set sails; scrubbed decks. Crew put to picking oakum. Quarrel between Tim and Dago Jack. Dinner: fish and potatoes. No whales, no whales at all. Nothing to do. Still calm.

Saturday: set sails; scrubbed decks. Lookout thought he saw a spout. Mistaken. Plum duff for dinner. Nothing in afternoon. Nothing, nothing, nothing. Still calm.

'By graminy,' David muttered gloomily to himself as he read this over on Sunday afternoon, 'I wish something would happen; I wish some...'

He looked up and could hardly believe his eyes. Could it be true? He shot a quick glance at the lookout. He was probably asleep. No one else seemed to be awake enough to notice what he had seen either. Yet he was sure of it; dead certain. There was land off the port bow. Dim and indistinct in the hazy distance was something which could only be land.

'I wished something would happen, and it has!' he exclaimed happily, looking again to make very sure of what he saw before calling out.

His excited cry awoke the ship, and Captain Hunter burst out of the companionway in a rage that he had not been called before.

'Land ho!' the lookout belatedly called from the mainmast. 'Two points off the starboard bow, sir.'

In a little while they were coasting along the shore of an island which in every respect conformed to David's views of what a South Sea island should look like. A strip of white coral beach, a line of palms, and beyond this inviting prospect a range of low, heavily wooded hills. The bright, green foliage had a freshness about it which delighted the boy after endless days when nothing was to be seen but the deep blue of the Pacific; he could smell the earth and growing things. Far down the coast he noted an inlet of the sea leading into a lagoon fringed with coconut palms.

'What do you think of that?'

David turned eagerly to Frank.

'Oh, gee, that looks great! Where are we? Do you think we'll get ashore?'

'I guess it's one of the Fijis,' answered the harpooner. 'Maybe we'll land; maybe we won't. The natives hereabouts ain't too friendly. But we got to get fresh water, and we sure need some green stuff. We'll be gettin' the scurvy if we don't have some soon. Maybe Captain Hunter will try some trade if any of the savages come out to the ship. But it's risky business. These islanders have captured a whaleship before this, and massacred its crew. I've heard tell they got some white men prisoners whom they make work for them like slaves.'

David pricked up his ears: white men held as slaves. Suppose Uncle Bob had landed on one of these islands?

When the Sea Turtle reached a point opposite the lagoon, Captain Hunter gave the order to take in sail and let go the anchor. The crew were then summoned aft.

'I'm goin' to send two boats ashore,' Captain Hunter said when the men were assembled. 'We've got to get water and fresh fruit. But we don't want any trouble with the natives. I once had a brush with 'em and once is enough. The men who go ashore have got to stick together and stay by their boats. If any natives turn up, we'll treat 'em friendly, but we'll let 'em know we're armed...'

'Here come some canoes!'

Around a bend in the lagoon could be seen four large war canoes heading out toward the Sea Turtle. There were a dozen or fifteen men in each of them, but such men as David had never before seen in his life. They wore nothing except narrow strips of cloth about their waists and their entire bodies were painted in glaring colors. Copper rings hung from their ears and from their noses; their hair was thick and fuzzy. They were paddling swiftly.

David felt a shiver go up his spine.

'By golly, they're savages, all right!' he exclaimed. 'I guess they're cannibals, too.'

When the canoes were within hailing distance of the Sea Turtle, they stopped short. A tall, fierce-looking savage who had been seated in the stern of one of them jumped up, unexpectedly revealing that he wore a tattered red shirt, and waved his arms.

'Me speak English!' he shouted. 'Me white man's friend!'

'We might see if they wanted to trade, Mr. Starbuck,' Captain Hunter said to his first mate. 'There ain't enough of 'em to make any real trouble. See if you can make that fellow understand we just want water and fresh fruit.'

'You got fruit, yams, coconuts?' called out Mr. Starbuck.

'Yes, yes,' answered the savage chieftain. 'You got tobacco, whiskey, cloth? We come aboard make trade.'

Suiting the action to the word, the savages paddled their canoes alongside the ship. The crews looking over the rail could see that they were heavily laden with tropical fruits, coconuts, yams, some other unusual vegetables, and even a few scraggly chickens. The natives appeared friendly enough. They apparently were not armed except for short knives.

'Three or four come aboard. Rest stay canoes,' ordered Mr. Starbuck.

'Yes, yes,' answered the chieftain eagerly.

In another minute half a dozen of the savages were on deck and those in the canoes were handing up the supplies which the Sea Turtle needed so badly. Mr. Starbuck gave the order to break out some of the articles which the whale-ship had brought along for trade. The vessel carried no firearms and no whiskey. Captain Hunter refused to trade in them. But she had a considerable store of extra tobacco, printed cloth, and iron nails which South Sea Islanders always wanted.

The first mate began bartering with the chief. The crew gathered about in an eager circle. Even Captain Hunter came down from the quarterdeck. Despite all warnings, no one paid any attention to the natives in the canoes ranged alongside the ship.

David was the first to notice what was happening. One by one the savages were sneaking aboard the vessel. One would climb quietly over the rail and then fade away inconspicuously behind a whaleboat. Then another would board the ship somewhere else, with stealthy, quiet movements. The boy was startled to see how many more than the half-dozen Mr. Starbuck had said could come aboard were actually on deck. Then he noticed that many of them carried short, ugly knives; a few had heavy-headed hatchets. His blood suddenly ran cold.

'Captain Hunter,' he whispered, 'there's a good many savages aboard; they're armed.'

Captain Hunter glanced about quickly.

At that moment a high-pitched yell was heard.

As if by a prearranged signal, the islanders aboard the ship made a rush for the waist where the crew were gathered; those still in the canoes clambered over the side. Their chief stepped back quickly and, whipping out a knife he had concealed beneath his incongruous-looking red shirt, lunged at Mr. Starbuck.

Things began to happen fast. Mr. Starbuck narrowly dodged the savage's knife, drew his pistol and fired point-blank at his assailant. Captain Hunter regained the quarter-deck; the crew instinctively rushed for the whaling racks.

In less time than it takes to tell, the natives were on them, brandishing their knives. But the sailors had their whaling weapons and thrust mercilessly at the frenzied savages with harpoons and lances. The scene was one of indescribable confusion. The officers on the quarterdeck did not dare fire into the tangled mass of struggling men. The clash of weapons, the piercing shrieks of the wounded, the angry shouts and curses of the fighting men, turned the quiet deck into pandemonium.

David found himself with a cutting-in spade in his hand desperately warding off the attack of a naked, horribly painted savage who was trying to get under his guard with his knife. Forced back against the rail, the boy made a quick thrust at him. The sharp blade of the spade cut across the native's wrist, almost severing his hand. With a wild cry the savage dropped his knife, sprang to the rail and jumped overboard.

David saw another of the natives on the point of bringing his hatchet down on Frank's head. With a warning shout he rushed forward. The big harpooner wheeled about just in time, and with a wide swing of his iron knocked his assailant flat.

'Work your way aft! Work your way aft!' bellowed Captain Hunter from the quarterdeck. 'Give us a chance to shoot the varmints.'

The seamen backed off as the natives pressed closer and closer. With cool courage, as if they were used to fighting off such onslaughts every day of their lives, they thrust and parried with their harpoons, lances, and spades. They were in the fight now, and almost enjoying it. Three of them were down; a dozen of the natives lay on the deck. Blood was flowing freely.

Emboldened by the crew's apparent retreat, the savages tried to rush the quarterdeck. Six of them broke away and dashed at the officers. Immediately three pistol shots rang out. Two of the natives fell, a third dropped his knife and grasped his side.

'Rush 'em, men! Give it to 'em!' cried Captain Hunter, quickly reloading his pistol. 'Stick 'em like pigs!'

The crew of the Sea Turtle gave a shout which silenced the savages' war whoops. Their whaling weapons flashed in the bright sun as they rushed forward. A pistol shot whizzed by David's ear and a burly native just in front of him toppled over to fall at his feet. He jumped over him to press his advantage; caught one man with a sideswipe of his spade which sent him reeling across the deck. The islanders were giving way now; fighting for their lives.

'No quarter! Cut 'em down!'

It was Mr. Starbuck, looking more cheerful than he had in months. He had thrown aside his smoking pistol to grab a lance as a quicker and more effective way of dealing with the situation.

Suddenly the native ranks broke. Their attack had failed. With a realization of the helplessness of their position, those that could rushed to the rail and leaped into their canoes. Almost before the seamen realized what had happened, they were paddling frantically toward shore. A volley of pistol shots pursued them, but while many of the crew would have liked to lower a whaleboat and take off, Captain Hunter would not allow it. It was enough that the Sea Turtle was saved.

XV

A RESCUE

The Rescue

Chapter XV

A RESCUE

THE Sea Turtle presented a gruesome sight after the natives had made their getaway. Hardly a man had escaped injury. Nursing a slashed arm which in the excitement of the fight he had not even known had been cut, David thought the deck looked all too much as it had after they had been cutting-in whales.

Two of the crew had been killed and half a dozen were so badly injured that Captain Hunter ordered them brought into the cabin, where, with the help of the two mates, he undertook to treat their cuts as best he could. But there was some satisfaction in noting that the toll among the savages had been far heavier. Five were dead and ten had been too seriously wounded to be able to escape. Among the latter was the chieftain who had spoken English. He lay on the deck groaning miserably.

When their own injured had had their cuts bound up, the problem of what to do with the wounded islanders had to be faced. It was decided to take them ashore and leave them where they might be found by their companions. This was a dangerous expedient, but Captain Hunter did not want them aboard ship; and he was not sufficiently brutal to adopt the suggestion that they be thrown overboard to sink or swim. He called for volunteers for the landing party.

David was among those who stepped forward and they started moving the injured savages into two of the boats. As the boy tugged at the heavy body of the chieftain, he noticed an unusual necklace about his neck. Among some sharks' teeth and broken shells was a thin piece of gold. It looked like the back of a watch. David fingered it curiously. That's what it was: the back of a watch. It had a name on it.

He jumped to his feet with excitement: the name was 'Robert Worth.'

In another minute he had seized the native by the shoulder and was roughly shaking him.

'Where did this watch come from? Where did you get it?'

'Ugh, ugh,' groaned the savage.

'You gotta understand,' David repeated stubbornly. 'Where did you get watch?'

Again the man groaned. Was he going to die without revealing the secret? Frantically the boy shook him. He must find out.

'Where watch come from?'

The native opened one eye; shuddered.

'Me no understand.'

David grabbed his knife, which lay near at hand on the deck, and held it to the chieftain's throat. He couldn't possibly have used it on the defenseless man, but he felt he must frighten him into telling what he knew, whatever the consequences.

'Cut your throat if you don't tell where watch come from.'

The savage's eyes rolled in terror. The sweat started up on his painted forehead. He groaned more deeply than ever.

'Watch come from sailor,' he whispered. 'Sailor my friend.'

'Where is he? Where is he?' David almost shrieked.

'He my friend. He live with me ashore.'

The chieftain waved his arm weakly toward the shore and then let it drop back helplessly to the deck. It was clear he had only a few moments to live.

David despaired of finding out anything more. He thought quickly. If the savage had got the watch from Uncle Bob, then Uncle Bob might still be a prisoner in the village of these natives who had attacked the Sea Turtle. It could not be far off. Uncle Bob was somewhere close at hand, hidden away. He jumped to his feet and ran to the cabin.

'Captain Hunter!' he called breathlessly. 'The savages have my uncle a captive in their village.'

Captain Hunter looked up from the seaman whose wound he was trying to bind up.

'Your uncle? What are you talkin' about?'

'My Uncle Bob. Captain Bob Worth. You know, I told you about him.'

He quickly gave an account of how he had seen the name on the watch and what the dying savage had said.

'Holy mackerel!' exclaimed Captain Hunter, straightening up. 'If those villains have got an American sailor captive, and if that sailor be Captain Bob Worth, we'll rescue him or my name ain't Obadiah Hunter. Ahoy there! Lower the starboard boat. We're goin' ashore. Come on, lad.'

In a few minutes two boats had been lowered, their crews heavily armed, and they were pulling rapidly toward shore.

Around the point the lagoon stretched away inland, and after about fifteen minutes' vigorous rowing, what appeared to be a native village was sighted half hidden in a grove of tall, waving coconut palms.

'Easy, lads,' called Captain Hunter. 'We got to look this over before we do anythin' foolish.'

But there was not a native in sight. Not a sign of one, although several canoes could be seen drawn up on the beach as they pulled slowly inshore. The two boats were grounded and, headed by Captain Hunter with David at his heels, the seamen crept cautiously up the beach toward the native huts.

'Looks as if they'd cleared out, lock, stock, and barrel,' muttered Captain Hunter.

The waves lapped softly on the beach, some monkeys chattered at them from the tops of the palms, and off in the distance a bright-colored parrot gave a harsh, discordant call. Otherwise there was not a sound to break the tropical quiet.

'Cleared out, by crackity!'

David was heartbroken as he followed Captain Hunter along the straggling line of native huts. What could they do? They couldn't follow the savages into the jungle. They would be ambushed too easily. Even if they weren't attacked, they would quickly get lost in the dank under-brush which crowded down to the edge of the clearing. Perhaps the natives had Uncle Bob with them; perhaps they had hidden him away somewhere.

The latter idea set him running feverishly from one hut to another. At the door to one of them he either heard, or imagined he heard, a feeble cry. He stood stock-still. Something was in there. Calling to Captain Hunter, he stuck in his head. At first he saw nothing. Then he caught sight of what looked like a heap of mats in one corner. Something moved. Another instant and he had pulled off the mats and was looking down at the emaciated figure of a white man.

He was so thin that his body looked like a skeleton. His hair was long and straggly; he wore a full beard. A strip of cloth about his waist served as his only covering; both his legs and arms were bound with thick palm fibers. As David looked at him, he opened his bloodshot eyes and groaned piteously.

'Water, water.'

As he called to his companions to come to his help, David did not really recognize the emaciated figure lying at his feet. He sensed rather than saw that it was his Uncle Bob. He remembered him so clearly as a hearty, sunburnt seaman, vigorously clapping him on the back as he told him that some day he'd take him on a whaling voyage. Could this pathetic skeleton really be his boyhood idol?

Captain Hunter had come into the hut and taken the situation in at a glance.

'The dirty hounds!' he muttered. 'I'd like to get my hands on 'em again. I'd show 'em, the dodgasted sons of sea cooks. But I hope we're in time. Here, there, we must get him aboard the Sea Turtle as quick as we can. Somethin' to eat and somethin' to drink, and he'll be right as a trivet. You can't kill a whaleman, by gar.'

Uncle Bob was picked up carefully and carried down to the boat. He did not seem to realize what was happening; he recognized no one. When the fetters were taken off his arms and legs, he did not have the strength to move them. Even after he had been given a drink, he kept feebly saying over and over again: 'Water, water.'

Captain Hunter had no desire to stay on shore a moment longer than he had to. Even though there was no sign of the savages about, they might return at any moment. Possibly they had gone off for re-enforcements. In any event, his idea was to get the victim of their cruelty aboard his ship as quickly as possible, and then get up the anchor and out of reach of any further attack. Leaving the wounded natives on shore, the two boats pulled back to the waiting ship.

Uncle Bob was tenderly hoisted aboard and carried to the cabin, while David routed up Sam to get some food and drink for him. Even before the boy reached the cabin, a dose of rum administered by Captain Hunter had caused some signs of returning consciousness to appear. As David entered, his uncle looked up and a puzzled look crossed his thin face.

'Why, it's Davey boy,' he said brokenly. 'Where in the merry blazes am I?'

'You're all right, Uncle Bob!' the boy cried joyfully. 'You're safe aboard the Sea Turtle. We'll be taking you home and . . .'

'Steady, lad,' interrupted Captain Hunter. 'Give him a chance to get somethin' to eat and drink before you start tellin' him your story. He'll be all right now. By gar, you can't kill a whaleman. Dern them bloodthirsty varmints!'

XVI

UNCLE BOB'S STORY

Uncle Bob Sights a Whaler

Chapter XVI

UNCLE BOB'S STORY

THE Sea Turtle did not attempt to make any further stops at the Fiji Islands after these exciting adventures, and it was not long before life aboard the whaleship became almost normal again. The crew had felt somewhat subdued when Captain Hunter somberly read the burial service over the bodies of the two men killed in the native attack, but on a whaling voyage death was not an altogether unexpected event. Nor did the seamen allow their injuries to trouble them very much — with the exception of Sam. He refused to let Captain Hunter touch his badly cut leg and consequently it healed very slowly.

David had been in Captain Hunter's cabin, called there to see his uncle, when the cook's turn to have his injuries looked over arrived. With Mr. Macy standing by to help him, Captain Hunter had washed the crew's cuts, occasionally taking a stitch or two, and clumsily bandaged them up.

Most of the men made no complaint, however roughly he dealt with them, but Sam, with a deep gash in his left leg, set up a howl.

'I'se hurt awful bad,' the big negro complained in a whining voice. 'I'se hurt awful bad. One of them savages jest about cut my leg off with his tomahawk. I'se got a rag round it, but it don't do much good. I guess I'll have to lay up awhile. I can't hardly move.'

'We'll see about that,' Captain Hunter said. 'Get up here on the table and let me see your leg.'

Sam climbed up and lay down, but, as Captain Hunter began to take off the dirty bandage, he sat up quickly.

'What's you goin' to do to it?'

'Here, there, lie down. I'm not goin' to hurt you.'

Captain Hunter pushed Sam back none too gently, and, with the bandage off his leg, began to swab the cut with a piece of cloth soaked in salt water.

The 'doctor' let out a howl and jumped up again.

'Will you lie down and stay down?' demanded Captain Hunter. 'What's the matter with you? You'd think you got hurt. It's only a scratch. It don't make no difference to me whether I fix you up. But since you're here I'm goin' to do it.'

Looking about, he saw David in the corner.

'Here, David,' he ordered, 'hold him down. If he jumps up any more, crack him over the head with a belayin' pin.'

Sam subsided grumbling, with a baleful look at David, but every time Captain Hunter touched his leg, he let out a howl and tried to get up. David clung to him as best he could, but was hardly heavy enough to keep him down. When Captain Hunter picked up a needle and thread, he gave a sudden spring which sent the boy reeling and almost knocked Captain Hunter over.

'I won't have no stitches in my leg!' he called back over his shoulder as he rushed for the companionway. 'I'se feelin' much better.'

David made a dive for him and started up the stairs, but Captain Hunter called him back.

'Let him go,' he ordered. 'His cut don't amount to much. If he don't want it bandaged, that's his hard luck. I'm no nursemaid. But just let me catch him loafin' on his job!'

Captain Hunter shook his head ominously; then turned to David.

'Your uncle's beginnin' to feel a bit better,' he said. 'He promised to spin his yarn. I thought you might like to hear it.'

Uncle Bob had been given a berth with Mr. Starbuck and was lying quietly in his bunk as Captain Hunter and David entered the cabin. He looked better than he had when rescued from the Fiji Islanders, but the nightshirt Mr. Starbuck had lent him hung loosely from his bony frame, his face was still thin and drawn and there was little color in his cheeks.

'Well, David,' he said in a rather feeble voice. 'So ye come to hear my yarn. It's nice of Captain Hunter to let yer sit down in the cabin along of two whaling captains. No foremast hand ever sat in my cabin, I tell ye. But I suppose as blood is thicker than water, it's all right for once. Don't let it go to yer head.'

'No, sir; no, Uncle Bob, I won't,' the boy answered, somewhat embarrassed. 'I'm sure Captain Hunter . . .'

'That's all right; that's all right,' broke in Captain Hunter. 'Let's get started with your tale, Captain Worth. How did those stinkin' niggers ever get hold of yer?'

'I'll start off right in the beginning, Captain Hunter,' answered Uncle Bob, 'and give ye the whole yarn.

'It's close on to two and a half years ago now, since the Rover went down. We'd had a fair cruise. Oh, there was some trouble. The crew had acted up one time and I'd put the ringleader in irons. He'd sailed with me before; I knew what kind he was. He'd have had the whole crew mutinyin' if I hadn't acted quick. Anyway, I clapped him into irons. That gave 'em all something to think about.

'We were somewhere off the Pelews, headed towards the offshore grounds. One night it blew up dirty weather. Yes, sir, it blew like the devil and then rained — rained as if it weren't ever goin' to stop. I couldn't get a sight. I knew we were getting off our course a bit, but I didn't know where we were. It'll let up in a day or so, I said to myself, and then we'll be all right. I hadn't turned in for three days, so I decided to go below and get some sleep.

'Just before I went off, it seemed to me by the motion of the ship that it was beginning to blow a bit harder. But my mate was as good a seaman as ye could find west of Cape Horn and that didn't worry me. I dropped into a quick sleep and was dreaming of home. Ye mind that apple orchard by your pa's house, David? I was dreaming of it that stormy night.

'Well, I'd just dropped off when a sharp crash sent me spinning out my bunk and half across the cabin. There was a terrible, ripping noise; the ship gave a sort of a lurch, and then slowly swung around. I could hear yelling and screeching on deck; the tear of canvas as the wind pulled at the sails, and the grinding of the planks in the ship's bottom. I knew she'd run on a reef. I grabbed my shirt and pants and rushed on deck.

'The mainmast snapped off like a twig just as I came out of the cabin and I've never seen such a sight as the deck of that ship. With the vessel keeled over almost on her beam ends and down at the stern, ye couldn't walk on deck. Ye had to crawl. And the waves were breaking over her like the flood. The foremast hands had run for the boats. They were trying to loose the falls on those which hadn't already been smashed.

' "Avast there!" I yelled. "Ye won't live for a moment in a sea like this."

'But they paid no attention to me. They got one boat lowered and ten men jumped into it as it lay there, banging against the ship's side. They shoved off. We saw a wave lift the boat high on its crest; then it dropped like a plummet. That's all we saw of it. We didn't see a one of the men again either.

'But it wasn't much better aboard the ship. She was startin' to break up. The sea was poundin' against her and ye couldn't tell how long she'd last. It was a chance whatever ye did. I told my mate to watch out for himself and he decided to lower another boat. But he tied a line about his waist and fastened it to a cleat.

' "Ye'll heave in on the line if we break up?" he asked, just as he got in the boat. I promised I would.

'But the boat was still fast when a wave hit it and smashed it against the side of the ship. Two of its crew clung to the falls and somehow the beggars managed to get back on deck. I jumped to the line tied about the mate and we pulled him aboard. Aye, we pulled him aboard, but he was unconscious. Maybe his head had struck something; he didn't come to at all.

'There were ten of us left aboard ship and only one boat. I sang out that I was going to wait till morning; that it was suicide to try to launch another boat. Then that seaman I'd had in irons before the wreck — you know, the one I told you wanted to start a mutiny — he yelled:

' "Wait till morning and be damned! We're going to launch this boat now and not be drowned like rats in a trap."

'But as he jumped for the boat, I jerked out my gun.

' "Ye'll follow orders now or get a shot in the head."

'He hesitated a moment; then saw I meant it, and stopped. I can see him yet, the beggar. He had a scar which stretched right across his cheek — an ugly scar. I'll never fergit the scoundrel!

'Anyway, there was only one boat left. It was bad enough aboard the ship. She was bound to break up soon. But the sea might go down before she did, and then was the time to try to launch the last boat.

'Well, sir, that's the way it worked out. By morning the sea had gone down. We could launch the boat. There were ten of us in it and all the supplies we could get aboard. That wasn't much. We had three or four hams, half a dozen pounds of bread, and four gallons of water. That's not a great deal for ten sailors when you're adrift in the middle of the Pacific.

'About a mile off was a low-lying rocky island. I don't yet know what it was. I was out of my position. But that island didn't do us any good. There warn't sign of a tree or shrub on it and there it was all by itself. Yes, sir, we were adrift in the middle of the ocean.

'I said the sea had gone down. Well, it had; otherwise we'd never've launched the boat. But it hadn't gone down enough to save the ship. She was breaking up as we pulled away.

'Those waves were the biggest I've ever seen. We'd ride up one side and plunge down the other. I tried to keep our head up into the wind, but it was the hardest work I've ever done. I don't know how we stood it; I don't know how long we stood it; but after a time it calmed down enough for us to take our bearings.

'There we was. Ten men in a boat with enough supplies for a week or two, on short rations. We'd no idea where the nearest land lay. I set a general course toward where I thought the Pelews ought to be; divided the crew into two watches; had a sail rigged up and the boat properly bailed. Then I told my crew I'd portion out supplies as I thought best. If anyone objected, I said, I'd shoot him dead on the spot.

' "We ain't got much chance, lads," I told 'em, "but the only chance we've got is to keep the course I've set ye just as long as we can. We ain't likely to speak another ship. The longer we make the supplies last, the more likely we'll reach land. One man's got to be in command; I'm that man. Ye'll do as ye're told."

'That was all right for everyone except this scar-faced fellow I'd had in irons. But it was chiefly for him I'd made my speech. I had my gun and didn't intend to have any trouble.

'We sailed in that little boat for fifteen days. There's not much to tell about it. Instead of rough weather and stormy seas, it turned hot as an oven. We didn't have enough food; we didn't have enough water. The sun was a ball of fire and our heads spun around with the fever of it. Our eyes started out of their sockets with the bright glare of the sea; our parched tongues stuck to the roofs of our mouths. We'd wash our faces in the brine, but it was hot. We wanted to drink that salty water so much it almost drove us mad. The men began to demand the last of the food; they called for the little water which was left. They muttered to themselves; they cursed and fingered their knives. I sat in the stern, night and day, gun in hand.

'Maybe I fell asleep; maybe I just slumped down exhausted in the bottom of the boat. I don't know yet what happened. It was the thirteenth day. We had so little left to eat or drink, it didn't seem to matter what happened. I remember I was lookin' for sight of a sail, and then I remember lying in the bottom of the boat with that mutineer's knife at my throat.

'I couldn't do a thing to save myself. It's just luck I lived to spin you the yarn. He'd made a jump for me and had me down. But the rest of the crew was just as anxious to get at the supplies: they didn't know how little there was left. The moment I was down they rushed aft. They knocked this fellow off me and while I lay there in the bottom of the boat, those nine starving men fought over me for a few loaves of bread and a couple of quarts of water. They clutched at the food and at each other's throats. They was mad with thirst and hunger.

'I don't know why they didn't do me in. That mutineer wanted to, but for some reason they wouldn't let him. I was left lying in the bottom of the boat. They'd taken my gun. I didn't much care what happened.

'Well, for two days we sort of drifted before the wind, the crew quarreling and cursing the whole time. Then we sighted land. It was a little island with a few straggling trees on it. The men at the oars hardly had the strength to pull toward it, but finally we drew up on shore. Water was what we wanted more'n anything else. I was so weak I crawled on my hands and knees looking for a spring. At last I found one. Nothing ever tasted so good in my life.

'But except for a couple of springs, we couldn't find anything on the island. We hunted for birds' nests, for crabs, for anything ye could eat. There warn't a thing.

'I was a little way inshore, by myself, and suddenly I thought I heard the boat being launched. As fast as I could I hurried back. Yes, sir, the boat was being launched. Another island lay a few miles off, and I guess the crew decided to make for it while they still had the strength. They was leaving me behind. I yelled at 'em to take me aboard; they didn't pay any attention. They left me there to starve.

'When I'd given up all hope of their turning back, there was nothing left to do. It's all up, I thought to myself. No more whalin' for Bob Worth. I went back near that spring and lay down.

'Just what happened the next few days I don't really know. I guess I went out of my head. I remember eating grass and chewing the bark off the trees. Then it must have been that some native canoes from another island came ashore and the savages in 'em must have found me and took me aboard. But it's all a sort of nightmare. I had a burning fever and nothing mattered.

'Several days later, I guess it was, I found myself lying on the ground in a native hut. I was so weak I could hardly move. Squatting near me was a fierce-lookin' savage with his whole body tattooed in weird designs and great copper rings in his ears and nose. For some time we sat staring at each other.

'"Me speak English."

'If I hadn't been so weak, I'd have jumped up. It gave me a start, I tell ye, to hear that painted heathen speak to me in my own language. I thanked him for having saved my life; I pleaded with him to continue his protection. For a long time he said nothing.

'"Me chief this island. White man my slave."

'At first I didn't understand what he meant. Then my heart sank. Perhaps it'd have been better if I'd starved on the island. I didn't know what was goin' to happen now.

'It was lucky I didn't. For more'n two years I've been that savage's slave. I was kicked about like a dog, made to work in the broiling sun without a piece of cloth to cover my blistered body, fed only scraps. There were times when I lay sick on the ground, burning with fever, and cried all night for water. If it looked as if I'd die, my master would bring me something to drink or something to eat; as soon as I had recovered, he would drive me out into the fields to work.

'One time I was out digging yams when I sighted a whaler headed straight for the island. You can imagine how I felt. All that night, as I lay on my mat in the chief's hut, I plotted how I could escape if the ship came in close to shore. If I could only get in touch with her crew, if I could only get word to the ship that I was a captive, I thought, they'd rescue me.

'The next morning the ship was in full sight. She was anchored just off the lagoon where you anchored, and there was a great powwow goin' on among the natives about what to do. I tried to keep out of sight so they'd forget me. There was no sign of a boat putting off from the whaler and finally the natives decided to send out some canoes. I hid away, thinking after they'd put off I'd steal a small canoe. Then I could paddle out toward the ship while they were busy trading.

'They went off. I stole a canoe and started out. No one noticed me. With my heart thumping so I could hardly breathe, I drew nearer and nearer the ship. Maybe someone would spot me for a white man. I didn't dare hail the ship too soon. The savages might recapture and kill me before any help could come. But I had almost decided to risk it when I heard something which made my blood run cold. It was the sound of a paddle right behind me.

'I jumped up and started to yell. But before I could utter a sound, the man who had chased me struck me across the side of the head with his paddle. I went over the side of the canoe like a tenpin. When I came up with my lungs full of water, he hit me again. That was the last I knew. I must have been dragged out of the water and taken ashore. If anyone aboard the whaler noticed it, there was no reason for him to guess I was a white man. When I came to this time, I was in the hut again, lying on a pile of mats. The whaleship had sailed away.

'After that I was treated worse than ever. Whenever the savages went away or whenever a ship was sighted, I was bound hand and foot and hidden away. I didn't know anything about the arrival of your ship. I didn't know she had come inshore or that the savages planned to capture her. I couldn't believe my senses when I saw ye in the hut.'

Uncle Bob buried his face in his hands. His whole body shook as if just the memory of what he had gone through was too much for him. Then he straightened up.

'That's my yarn, that's the whole of it,' he said. 'I guess I don't need to tell ye how grateful I am to ye, Captain Hunter. Now if ye'll give me a chance, I'd like to earn my passage home. I thought some day I'd be taking David here on a voyage, but it seems like things are backward and he's taking me home.'

'Don't go worryin' about anythin' like that,' Captain Hunter answered heartily. 'I'm glad to help a fellow whaler whenever I can. I'll sign you up as third mate and you can rest up until you get your full strength back. We're glad to have you aboard, ain't we, David?'

David hardly knew what to say. He had listened to his uncle with his eyes immovably fixed on that thin, worn face; he could not realize that it was Uncle Bob telling this incredible tale of shipwreck, mutiny, and savage cruelty, here aboard the Sea Turtle, the boy's own ship.

'Yes, sir; yes, sir,' he said at length in answer to Captain Hunter's question. 'Thank you, sir.'

Captain Hunter looked at the boy's rapt face quizzically, and then got up from the table where they had been sitting.

'All right, lad; get along forrard where you belong.'

David left, still in something of a daze, but that night he was telling an attentive forecastle the whole tale of his uncle's adventures. And it lost nothing in the telling.

XVII

AMBERGRIS

Ambergris

Chapter XVII

I T WAS not until he was in his bunk that night that David suddenly thought of Dago Jack. The moment his uncle had mentioned that the mutinous sailor had a strange scar across his face, he had known that the man was his enemy aboard the Sea Turtle. Then in the excitement of hearing of shipwreck and savage captivity, he had forgotten all about it. But putting things together, he was certain that he had been right in his first guess.

'By graminy!' he exclaimed half aloud, sitting up in his bunk with a jerk. 'By graminy, that goldarned Portuguese is the man who did his best to murder Uncle Bob!'

He'd see to it that Dago Jack paid for it, the boy thought to himself. But what should he do? Had he better jump right up now and tell Captain Hunter? At first he thought that was what he ought to do, and started to pull on his boots. Then he realized there was no hurry. There was no chance of Dago Jack escaping while the Sea Turtle was at sea.

The first thing in the morning would do, the boy decided, and then the Portuguese would find out what it was like to be put in irons. It would be a good thing for the ship to have him out of the way. David had to admit that Dago Jack was all right on the whaling grounds or in a brush with natives, but just as his uncle had said, he was always stirring up trouble among the men before the mast. David felt sure he would have them mutinying again unless something was done about it.

The next morning he sought out the Captain.

'Captain Hunter.'

'Well?'

'You know that man my uncle was telling us about, the one who tried to kill him when they were at sea in the whaleboat?

'Yes.'

'He's aboard the Sea Turtle.'

'Aboard the Sea Turtle? What are you talkin' about, lad? What kind of a yarn is this?'

'It's Dago Jack.'

'Dago Jack? What makes you think it's Dago Jack?'

'Remember Uncle Bob said as how the man had a scar across his cheek? I know it's him.'

'You're crazy, lad; there's plenty of seamen got scars. That's no reason. Why, he'd barely have had time to get back to New Bedford and ship again.'

'I know, but I'm sure it's him just the same. If you'd let Uncle Bob see him...'

Captain Hunter looked at the boy quizzically. He was very much in earnest, very determined. A dim suspicion crossed the old whaler's mind that perhaps he was right.

'That Dago Jack's an ugly customer,' he muttered, half to himself. 'It wouldn't be beyond him. I'll have him brought aft.'

He sent for the Portuguese, and when he appeared, ordered

him without a word of explanation to come down into the
cabin. David followed and was standing just behind them
at the open door to the stateroom where Uncle Bob was
lying in his bunk.

He saw his uncle look up and his face suddenly darken.

'Where'd you spring from, you dirty scoundrel?' Uncle
Bob exclaimed fiercely, struggling to get up. 'By God, I'll
teach you...'

But it was too much for him. He fell back feebly.

Dago Jack made no move as he stood there, confronted
by the man he had tried to kill and then marooned on a
desert island, but Captain Hunter quickly grabbed hold
of him.

'Is this the man you was tellin' us about?' he asked Uncle
Bob.

'That's the dirty scoundrel as tried to kill me,' Uncle Bob
answered weakly. 'Sure as my name's Bob Worth.'

'By the great horn spoon, if that don't beat the Dutch!
Why you dodgasted son-of-a-gun! We'll have you strung
up fer that. Mr. Starbuck' — turning to the mate who had
followed them below in some curiosity — 'did you hear
that? Put this man in irons. He'll stay in 'em until we reach
port. Then we'll hand him over to an American consul.
Mutiny and attempted murder, by gosh!'

Dago Jack didn't say a word and made no resistance when
Mr. Starbuck took hold of him and marched him up on
deck. He shot a vengeful look at David, but the boy met
his glance squarely. Nevertheless, he couldn't help wondering whether this was really the final end of the long feud
which had started so long ago at the Crossed Harpoons.
Somehow he felt that he had not seen the last of Dago Jack,
that something further was bound to happen. He didn't

know what. With the Portuguese in irons, he could hardly start a mutiny. Just the same, David decided, he'd keep a careful watch on Spider and Heinie in case they should try to communicate with the prisoner.

Events were to prove that David's suspicions were well founded. In the meantime, however, the hunt for whales continued and they had a run of fairly good luck. Several were taken and a quantity of good sperm oil stowed away below decks. At one lowering a boat was swamped when an ugly bull whale turned on it and two of the crew were dragged out of the water badly shaken up, but otherwise there was for a long time no special excitement.

When the lookout sang out late one afternoon that he had sighted another whale, the crew consequently prepared to lower with the easy skill of long practice. This whale, however, was not spouting and the way its huge body rolled in the swells indicated that it was probably dead. Captain Hunter ordered only one boat lowered and David found himself in his old place in Mr. Starbuck's boat.

If there had been any question about the whale's being dead, it was quickly answered. The boat crew realized not only that it was dead, but that it was very dead. Coming up on it, the terrific smell of the carcass told the whole story. The body exuded a horrid, nauseating stench which made David feel positively sick.

It had been partly eaten away by sharks, and, as Mr. Starbuck ordered the men to stop pulling, the boy wondered whether he might not perhaps decide that there was not enough oil left to make it worth trying-out. But he noticed that the mate was gazing at the whale with a curiously intent look.

'What's the matter?' the boy asked the oarsman next to him.

'I dunno,' he answered. 'Maybe he thinks there's amber-gris.'

'Ambergris? What's that?'

'What's ambergris? Well, I dunno as I can really tell ye. It's a funny sort of stuff, yellow and sticky. It comes from a whale's insides. Sometimes when you cut one up, you find it in his belly; sometimes you come across it floatin' on the sea. It stinks to heaven.'

'Why's Mr. Starbuck bothering about stuff like that?'

'It's worth a lot of money, lad. They use it makin' per-fume, I've heard tell. When you mix it with other things, it makes them smell sweeter. Ain't that queer? You get this ambergris out of a stinkin' dead whale and you use it to make perfume for ladies to put on their clothes or some-thin'. Yes, sir, it's worth a lot of money. If we find some, it'll mean bigger lays for all of us.'

'Golly, I hope there's some in this whale, then,' David said, peering closely at the whale toward which they were drifting closer and closer. 'Why don't we pull in nearer? Hey, could that be it?'

His sharp eyes had caught sight of something which looked like a piece of overripe cheese. It was a thick glob of yellowish stuff, floating close to the carcass. He pointed at it excitedly.

'By gosh, it's ambergris!' one of the crew exclaimed. 'Here's somethin' worth getting hold of, however much it stinks.'

'Fer the love of Heaven!' said another softly. 'It'll be handsome lays for us if that's the real thing.'

Mr. Starbuck, no less excited than his crew, had swung the boat around and they now pulled toward the bobbing treasure until it was almost within reach. The smell of the whale was almost overpowering, a stench that was like nothing else on land or sea, but it was almost forgotten. Mr. Starbuck took an oar and carefully worked the floating mass alongside the boat and then, leaning over the side, looked it over carefully. The crew watched him anxiously.

'Yes, sir; it's ambergris, all right.'

The seamen let out a whoop, clapped each other on the back, and broke out in a chorus of exclamations.

'Holy catfish, what a haul! What a lucky chance!'

'That means good lays for us. By crackity, I'll enjoy spending what that brings in.'

It took them some time to get the ambergris into the boat. It must have weighed about twenty-five pounds. Then, after poking about a little, several more pieces were found. In their excitement the crew forgot about the sickening smell which a little while before had almost overcome them. When they drew up beside the whale to let Mr. Starbuck see if there could possibly be any more of the stuff inside the decaying carcass, every man that could grabbed an iron or lance to jab hopefully at the rotting blubber. But it was soon clear that they had found all the ambergris there was.

'What's it worth? What's it worth?' David asked eagerly, when at last they were ready to pull back toward the waiting ship.

'Golly, I never seen so much in my life,' the next oarsman answered. 'I've heard of it bringin' more'n hundred dollars a pound. We got sixty pounds, maybe. What would that be?'

'Whew!' whistled David. 'A hundred dollars a pound! Why, we'd have about six thousand dollars!'

He was staggered by the thought of so much money. Could that smelly stuff really be worth so much? As they pulled back toward the ship, he thought of the many ways he could spend his share of it.

Long before they reached the Sea Turtle, the rest of the vessel's crew knew that something unusual had happened by the speed with which the boat was returning. The rail was lined with curious and expectant faces.

'What is it, Mr. Starbuck; what is it?' called Captain Hunter as soon as the boat was within hailing distance.

'Ambergris, sir. A good haul,' the mate shouted back.

'Are you sure?'

'Yes, sir. No doubt about it. There's almost sixty pounds of it.'

The men let out a cheer and as the boat drew alongside, they gladly helped in getting the stuff aboard. Captain Hunter looked it over carefully. He smelled it; felt its weight.

'Good work, Mr. Starbuck, good work,' he said at last. 'That's the best haul of ambergris I've ever seen. It ought to be worth a good deal. We'll make a voyage now all right — unless somethin' goes wrong.'

He ordered the ambergris taken to the cabin; then turned back.

'Call the crew aft, Mr. Starbuck.'

The order was hardly necessary. The men were gathered in the waist of the ship.

'You all know what this means,' Captain Hunter addressed them. 'We got about sixty pounds of ambergris; it ought to fetch a good price when we get back to New Bedford. You can thank Mr. Starbuck here for your good luck.

'But don't go spendin' your money until you get it. We ain't home yet. And we're not headin' that way until we get a full ship, ambergris or no ambergris. We're out for oil and we're goin' to hunt whales just as if we hadn't found this stuff. I don't want any sojerin' because you think you've got a good lay comin' to you already. You'll work or you'll get discharged at the next port for refusin' duty.'

With this little speech he disappeared down the companionway. The ambergris was going to be carefully locked up.

'I'm derned!' muttered one of the hands. 'We find that there ambergris and he tells us we'll be discharged if we don't work harder'n ever. We got enough oil to head for home now that that stuff's aboard, too.'

'By crackity, you're right,' chimed in another. 'What's the good of spendin' the rest of our lives huntin' whales when we got somethin' in the cabin there that's worth more oil than we'd get in months?'

'Cheer up, mates,' broke in Frank. 'We'll soon have the ship full and be headin' toward the Cape. What are you grousin' for? You'd think we'd lost a whale instead of findin' somethin' better.'

'What good's it do us?' growled Heinie, taking heart from the grumbling tone of his shipmates' comments to pick up his old habit of complaining. 'I bet we never see that stuff again. I bet the Old Man sells it for himself and we don't get any bigger lays than we would have, anyway.'

'That's right.' Spider now edged his way into the little knot of discontented seamen who seemed to feel most keenly Captain Hunter's talk of being discharged. 'I've heard of captains treatin' their crew that way. I won't put up with it, for one.'

David was surprised at the sudden turn of events. He, too, had been disappointed that the lucky find would not mean they would be sailing homeward any sooner. He had had the feeling that now the voyage would be quickly over. He had thought of landing at New Bedford and proudly going home with Uncle Bob. He had imagined the happy welcome from his family and their astonishment at the story of his uncle's rescue. But he didn't like the grumbling of the crew; he particularly didn't like the sinister hints of Heinie and Spider.

'It's a lucky thing Dago Jack's in irons,' he thought to himself. 'Otherwise he'd be stirring up real trouble. He almost got the crew to mutiny once. With this new grievance, he might be able to get them to follow his lead again.'

As he went slowly forward, the boy saw that some of the malcontents were still grumbling, cursing Captain Hunter for his failure to promise them a speedy homeward voyage. Heinie and Spider seemed to be egging them on. The latter's little eyes glanced craftily about the deck as he whispered something to one of the crew. David felt that trouble was brewing even though Dago Jack was not on hand to foment it.

XVIII

TROUBLE BREWING

Conspirators

Chapter XVIII

TROUBLE BREWING

THERE was no doubt the next few days that a good many of the crew felt as Heinie and Spider did. Discontent was rife in the forecastle; almost everyone was grumbling. Nor did it help matters that no whales were sighted. Life aboard the Sea Turtle settled down again into that tedious humdrum which several times previously on the long voyage had threatened to lead to trouble.

Heinie and Spider found it easy to instill new grievances into the minds of the foremast hands. They were forever complaining, cursing Captain Hunter and both mates, sowing seeds of suspicion as to what might be done with the ambergris so carefully locked away in the cabin.

David himself found it hard to remain cheerful. He, too, felt a grievance. He would have liked to talk it over with his uncle, but Captain Bob still kept to his cabin.

'How much longer do you think the voyage'll last?' he asked Frank one day as he was coiling the whalelines and making things generally shipshape in one of the boats.

'So you're beginnin' to grumble, too!' said Frank, with a quick glance at the boy.

David flushed.

'No, I'm not exactly grumbling, but if this ambergris is so valuable, what's the use of cruising, cruising, cruising...'

'Stow it,' the harpooner broke in. 'It's natural for the likes of Spider and Heinie to start chawin' about that sort of thing. Probably Dago Jack put 'em up to it just to make trouble. But I thought I was makin' a whaleman out of you.

'Look here. We came out to get oil, didn't we? We've had good luck. Dern good luck, if you count the ambergris. But there's still a lot of empty casks in the hold. It's Captain Hunter's job to get them filled and it's our job to follow orders. I think he's figurin' on visitin' the off-shore grounds again. If we have any luck there, we might fill the ship up. Then we're on our way home. The Sea Turtle will be roundin' Cape Horn before you know it.'

'What about supplies?' David asked. 'We didn't get much at the Fijis and now we're running out of water.'

'You'd think you was in command,' Frank said sarcastically. 'Don't you worry. The Old Man knows what he's about. I wouldn't be surprised if we called at the Marquesas or Washington Island. We'll get shore leave, too.'

'I bet we don't,' the still discouraged boy answered.

'Sure we will. Why do you think whalin' captains don't like to give their crews shore leave? Because they're afraid they'll desert. When a crew gets grousin' they're like to make for the woods and not show up when the ship's ready to sail. Even when they're kept on shipboard, there're a lot of fools who'll try to make off in a boat. They'll even take a chance with the sharks in swimmin' ashore. Anything to get on land again and away from their ship. They just get plumb tired of the sea.

'We were off the Friendly Islands once. Four men made

a raft and started to float ashore one night. Someone gave the alarm. A boat was lowered. We put off after 'em. Just as we was about to overtake 'em they slipped off into the water. It was a dark night; we couldn't see much. But we heard a great splashin' and a horrible screamin'. The sharks don't need no lights.

'But nothin' like that'll happen this time, lad. Captain Hunter'll give us liberty and you can bet your last penny every man-jack of us will be settin' on the beach there waitin' for a boat when it comes time to sail.'

'Why?'

'Because of that there ambergris. The voyage's almost over, whatever happens, and that stuff means good lays. Nobody'll want to be throwin' that over. You're in luck, lad, and you don't know it. Cheer up now. We'll be gettin' ashore soon and you'll be able to stretch your legs and get the feel of land again. Then before you know it, we'll be roundin' Cape Horn and there'll be New Bedford town comin' in sight. Your pa'll probably be on the dock waitin' for ye.'

He gave the boy a hearty slap on the back and left him at his work.

Thinking over what Frank had said, David began to feel a little ashamed of himself for grumbling. He didn't want to be like Heinie and Spider. He wasn't going to help them stir up trouble. It would be fun to get ashore and feel land under his feet. He started whistling.

But while Frank had succeeded in reconciling David to a long voyage, his shipmates became continually more rebellious. The ambergris seemed to exercise a sinister influence over the forecastle. There were continual quarrels among the crew about nothing at all; continual grumbling about the food; continual cursing of the officers. One man talked back to Mr. Starbuck and only a swift blow from that rough-and-ready seaman taught him better manners, while another time Captain Hunter threatened to seize up and flog a man who was slow about obeying an order. That night there was muttered talk in the forecastle of 'showin' them slave-drivers what kind of men we are.'

On deck a few nights later, when the Sea Turtle was at last drawing near to the Marquesas, David felt a certain tenseness in the air. When he saw Spider furtively slip around the after deck-house and join a little group of sailors gathered there in the shadows, he decided to draw up on them and try to discover what was going on. They had the air of conspirators; he knew that if he joined them openly he would learn nothing.

Very quietly he crept around by the try-works, out of sight of them, but close enough to be able to hear what might be said. They were talking in low tones.

'I'll get him; I'll lay the buzzard out with a belayin' pin,' David heard one of the seamen say, the man whom Captain Hunter had threatened to flog. 'The old fool can't have me seized up for nothin' at all!'

'Shut up, you're talkin' too loud,' Spider broke in. 'We're goin' to stick together on this, see? If you start anythin' too soon, we won't be able to get away with it.'

'All right, all right,' the man answered grumpily. 'But when's somethin' goin' to start?'

'Any day now. He's just waitin' to be sure. He knows what he's doin'. When I went below last night he said...'

David could not quite hear the rest of Spider's sentence. Who was 'he'? What was being planned? He was about to edge closer to the little group of sailors when he felt himself suddenly seized by the arm in a grip so fierce that he cried out involuntarily.

'Keep your mouth shut,' someone muttered in his ear, 'or I'll fix you so's you can't never open it again.'

For a horrible moment, the boy thought it was Dago Jack. If it had been, he did not doubt that the Portuguese would have killed him. But it was not Dago Jack; it was Heinie. The German had caught him trying to overhear their conversation and now dragged him around the try-works to where Spider and the rest were gathered.

'Look what I found,' he said, 'hidin' here in the dark.'

'Why are you stickin' your nose in somewhere it don't belong?' muttered one of the seamen. 'By thunder, we'll teach you your manners. You'll try to spy on us, will ye?'

He drew back his arm as if to hit the boy, but Spider quickly interposed.

'Cut that out, you goldarned fool. Didn't I tell you to keep your mouth shut?' Spider's tone was angry, but he turned toward the boy with an attempt at a smile. 'Why, it's David. We were just talkin' about how soon we'd be turnin' toward home. It seems like we ought to be gettin' along.'

David didn't know what to say or do as Heinie relaxed his grip and the seamen eyed him suspiciously. He knew something was afoot; he didn't know just what. But it was clear that under the circumstances it would be better to pretend he had not overheard even the little that he had.

'What are you threatening me about?' he exclaimed. 'I ain't the captain or the mate either. I'm just as anxious to get home as any of you. I don't want to spend the rest of my life cruising around the Pacific when we already got a good cargo.'

Spider looked at him closely. The boy's tone somewhat disarmed his suspicion, but he apparently had no idea of continuing the interrupted conversation. Whatever was being plotted, it was not for David's ears. The group of sailors gradually broke up, and after a time the boy found himself alone.

He had not been deceived by the conspirators' attempted friendliness. He knew that Spider had been trying to cover his tracks and prevent anyone else from saying anything which might give away what he really was going to do. David was determined to watch him more closely than ever. Somehow he felt that Dago Jack was involved in it all, with Spider acting as his lieutenant.

For the next few days nothing further happened. There was grumbling; there were mysterious conversations among the malcontents. One time David overheard Spider say something about the ambergris. But every time he came near any of Spider and Heinie's followers, they shut up. David tried in vain to get some further clue as to what was going on.

All the time Dago Jack was in irons and confined to the ship's run, a narrow, dark space between decks where he could be kept in solitary confinement. Three times a day someone took him his food, but otherwise none of the crew was supposed to have any contact with him. One day David was deputed to take him his rations.

As he drew near the Portuguese, he noticed that there was someone with him. David stepped behind an oil barrel and peered around it. As his eyes gradually adjusted themselves to the darkness, he recognized the slim outline of Dago Jack's visitor. It was Spider. As David watched from his crouching position, he clearly saw Spider furtively hand something over to Dago Jack. The latter took it and hid it beneath his coat. A moment later Spider brushed past the boy.

David gave Dago Jack his food without a word.

The incident troubled him, however, more than anything else that had happened so far. He knew now that Dago Jack must be behind whatever it was that was being plotted. What could Spider have given him? Should he have accused Spider then and there? Should he report his suspicions to Captain Hunter? He decided to tell Frank and see what the harpooner advised.

It was not he who sought out Frank, but Frank who sought him later that same day. The harpooner quietly called him aside.

'I've got somethin' for you to do secretly,' he said in a low voice. 'There's trouble in the forecastle. Real trouble. Have you heard anythin' suspicious?'

'Yes, I have,' David answered eagerly. 'Spider and Heinie and some of the others are plotting something, and Spider's been talking to Dago Jack.'

He quickly told Frank of the conversation he had overheard and was starting to tell of the meeting between Spider and Dago Jack when Frank interrupted him with a sudden exclamation.

'By the great horn spoon, that's it!' he said. 'You saw Spider hand somethin' over to Dago Jack? Did you see what it looked like?'

'No, I couldn't see,' the boy answered. 'It was something small. Dago Jack slipped it under his coat. I was going to tell you about it because it looks like . . .'

'Could it have been a pistol?' Frank again interrupted.

'Yes, I guess it could. But where would Spider have got a pistol?'

'Listen: what I was goin' to ask you to do was to search through the forecastle. I couldn't do it myself without givin' too much away. Captain Hunter's just missed a pistol. He kept it hanging up in his cabin. It's gone. Somebody's stolen it. That means trouble; it means mutiny.'

David's eyes shone with excitement.

'And you think Spider's stolen the pistol and slipped it over to Dago Jack? Yes, yes, that would be it. Spider said they were going to stick together and talked about someone who was just waiting to be sure. They're plotting to get Dago Jack free, and then . . .'

'And then they'll be using that pistol. You say you heard something about the ambergris?'

'Yes. It was Spider again, and Heinie. They were talking about the ambergris.'

'That's what they'd be up to. Work off their grudge against the officers and then steal the ambergris and get away while we're close to the Marquesas. By golly, maybe you've saved the ship by hearin' and seein' what you did. We got to let Captain Hunter know about this right away. Otherwise those villains will be breakin' out before we know it.'

David and Frank started aft.

XIX

MUTINY

The Mutineers

Chapter XIX

MUTINY

CAPTAIN HUNTER, Mr. Starbuck, and Mr. Macy were all three on the quarterdeck as David and Frank approached. It was a quiet afternoon. The Sea Turtle was sailing slowly with a gentle following breeze. Far off on the horizon was a faint blur which might well have been land, for they were nearing the Marquesas. The officers were at the rail, trying to make out what it was.

'Captain, can we have a word with you?' asked Frank.

Captain Hunter wheeled about quickly.

'Have you found that pistol?' he demanded brusquely.

'No, sir,' Frank answered, 'but young David here says as how he saw Spider handin' somethin' over to that skunk Dago Jack. It might have been a pistol . . .'

'What's that?'

'It might have been a pistol,' David said, a bit breathlessly. 'I heard Spider and Heinie and some of the others talking, sir. It sounded like they meant trouble, sir, and I think Dago Jack's behind it all. I didn't know you'd lost any pistol, but I saw Spider give something to Dago Jack just about the size of a pistol, and from the way they been talking, that's probably what it was.'

'What did they say?'

'One of 'em said something about laying you out with a belayin' pin, sir, and then Spider said they'd all have to stick together and something was going to start soon.'

'Wait 'til I get my hands on 'em,' Captain Hunter growled fiercely. 'I'll teach 'em. I'll seize 'em up and flog every dern one of 'em. Did they say anythin' more?'

'No, sir, that's about all. But I did hear Spider say something about the ambergris.'

'So they're worryin' about that, hey? They'll like to lay me out and then get hold of the ambergris. Well, I've seen mutiny before and I know how to deal with it. I'll make 'em toe the line or know the reason why. Who do they think's in command of this ship?'

He looked at David inquiringly, but the boy thought the question hardly needed an answer. After a moment's pause, the Captain continued:

'Yes, by Jupiter, I'll teach 'em! I'll . . . Look here. You keep your eyes and ears open, lad. If you hear anythin' more, come straight to me with it. You done well; you done very well.'

With a serious glint in his eye, he turned to his first mate:

'Mr. Starbuck, I want you to go with Frank and get that pistol back from Dago Jack. Don't make any fuss about it, just get it back. Then get hold of Spider and Heinie and bring 'em aft. I'll give 'em a lesson. When you've got 'em, call all hands on deck.'

He turned on his heel, and Mr. Starbuck and Frank started off. Left to himself, David went slowly back to the forecastle. It was a lucky thing he'd seen and heard what he had, he thought to himself. It was just in time. Now Captain Hunter could head off the mutiny before real trouble started. He was glad it was his warning that had made it possible.

As he started down the forecastle ladder, he thought he saw Spider hurrying across the almost deserted deck. But he wasn't sure. It didn't worry him, in any event. He knew that Mr. Starbuck would soon be taking care of him.

Going over to his bunk, however, he heard the sound of running feet on the deck above and stopped short in surprise. What could that be? He hurried up on deck again.

Just as he emerged from the hatchway, he saw Frank stagger up on deck, the blood flowing from a cut in the side of his head.

'He got away from us!' the harpooner bellowed at the top of his lungs. 'Dago Jack's got away with the pistol! Look sharp, Captain Hunter, he's . . .'

The warning came too late. At that instant David saw Dago Jack, with Spider and Heinie at his heels, rush onto the quarterdeck. As Captain Hunter whirled about from the rail, where he was standing with Mr. Macy, the Portuguese crashed the butt of the pistol down on his head with tremendous force. The Captain's knees sagged under him and he sank limply to the deck. Mr. Macy sprang to his defense, but a blow from Heinie sent him, too, staggering and stunned, against the bulwark.

So quickly had the attack taken place that the few sailors on deck had no time to realize what was happening, and before anyone could do anything, Dago Jack had swung about with his pistol in his hand.

'First man to move is dead,' he said grimly. 'I'm runnin' things now. What I say goes.'

After a moment of stunned surprise, David had started toward the quarterdeck. Now he stopped. He noticed that some of the crew had seized whaling weapons; the rest seemed too dazed to move. It was clear that a good many were in the plot, and that the others, especially those who had been below when Captain Hunter had been felled, were too surprised and frightened to be able to offer any resistance. With both Captain Hunter and Mr. Macy lying unconscious on the deck, Mr. Starbuck nowhere in sight, and Frank groggy from the blow on his head, there was no leadership for the men who might still be loyal. The mutineers had acted so quickly that they had got control of the ship before anyone suspected that an attack was under way.

'You understand?' Dago Jack was saying in an insolent, brazen voice. 'I'm in command here. Obey my orders and you'll be all right; disobey orders and you'll go overboard. But we ain't goin' to waste any time huntin' whales, I tell you. Not with this here ambergris in the cabin. If there's anybody here has any objections, he'll get what's comin' to Captain Hunter and the mates. I won't stand no foolishness from anyone.'

He glared fiercely at the men gathered in the waist of the ship. Some of them looked cheerful and expectant; others were glum and distrustful. But not a one moved.

'Now, you sons-of-guns who've always been so nice and friendly with them buzzards on the quarterdeck, line up here where I tell you.'

He singled out a number of hands who he knew were not likely to fall in with his scheme, and made them line up along the rail. David, not unexpectedly, found himself shoved in among them.

'You're goin' to be roped up until we decide what to do with ye,' he said brutally. 'Maybe you'll go the way the officers are goin'; maybe you won't. Spider, and you there, Heinie, get busy.'

Looking about David saw no possible escape. The mutineers were in complete command of the ship. If he made a move, he knew that Dago Jack would shoot him down without a minute's hesitation. He would probably be glad to do so. The boy's heart was beating furiously, and when he saw Dago Jack coming across the deck, eyeing him malevolently, he had a sudden sick feeling. He saw the swarthy Portuguese draw near, the livid scar across his cheek giving an even more sinister expression to the cruel smile which played about his thin lips, and remembered how often Dago Jack had threatened to get even with him before the voyage was over.

'So you would try to double-cross me, you dirty little rat,' muttered Dago Jack. 'Well, I've got you where I want you now. There'll be no Frank or Mr. Macy or Captain Hunter steppin' in to protect you either. I'll teach you to interfere with me.'

He stepped closer; then turned to Spider.

'Here, hand me that rope's end.'

He shifted his pistol to his left hand and, taking the heavily knotted piece of rope which Spider handed him, drew back his arm.

David stiffened to receive the expected blow; then caught sight of something which gave him a wild feeling of hope. At the cabin companionway he saw Uncle Bob. No one had thought of him, but hearing the commotion on deck, he had crawled from his bunk and now came staggering feebly out on deck, his face pale and drawn. He was standing directly behind Dago Jack, blinking his eyes in surprise at the sight before him.

In that split second, while Dago Jack's arm was poised over his head, David had a flash of inspiration. He saw his one chance.

'Uncle Bob!' he shouted. 'Shoot! Shoot!'

Dago Jack spun about with a snarl to face the newcomer. David wasted no time. With all his force he threw himself against the Portuguese. He caught him just above the knees and Dago Jack crashed to the deck, the pistol clattering out of his hand. The boy seized the pistol and sprang to his feet. The Portuguese, too, was up and on him like a tiger. David caught the sharp gleam of a knife. Almost automatically he pulled the trigger. A sharp report and Dago Jack slumped down.

Still dazed, the boy stepped back, and just then Spider rushed at him with a whaling lance. There was another pistol shot. The lance dropped from Spider's hand. He grabbed his arm with a cry of pain.

'Make for the quarterdeck!'

It was Frank's voice. Never had David been more glad to hear it. He saw him with a smoking pistol in his hand, blood still streaming from his head, stumbling across the deck.

Just as most of the crew had been taken entirely by surprise when Dago Jack and Spider had laid out the officers on the quarterdeck, so were the mutineers now caught off their guard by this quick turn in events. They watched Frank and David as if stupefied. Heinie stood dumbfounded, his mouth hanging open, unable to move without either Dago Jack or Spider to tell him what he should do.

With his pistol reloaded, Frank took command of the situation.

'Put your weapons away!' he ordered the crew, with an authority oddly at variance with his usual good nature.

The mutineers hesitated. Heinie appeared about to say something.

'If there's a man on deck with a harpoon or lance in his

hand in another two minutes,' the harpooner roared, 'I'll shoot him dead where he stands.'

He swayed a little on his feet as he spoke, but the hand holding the pistol was steady. He meant exactly what he said; the crew knew it.

Sullenly the mutineers put their weapons back on the rack. Spider, still holding his injured shoulder, cursed volubly; Heinie muttered gloomily to himself, but made no move. The inert body of Dago Jack lay where it had fallen. David's bullet had gone home. The Portuguese would never lead another mutiny.

Fortunately for David and Frank, they soon had re-enforcements. Even though they had so completely turned the tables on the mutineers, one of them was badly wounded and the other only a boy. If the crew had rushed them, they might not have been able to stand their ground for very long. But neither Captain Hunter nor Mr. Macy had been killed by the blows which had knocked them unconscious. With keen relief, David heard the Captain moan and saw the second mate struggling to his feet.

'I'll watch these skunks,' Frank whispered in the boy's ear. 'You see what you can do for Captain Hunter and Mr. Macy.'

One of the crew spoke up.

'We ain't in this thing,' he said. 'We got no hand in Dago Jack's mutiny. We'll tie up these sons-of-guns and have things shipshape again in no time.'

'All right,' said Frank.

He ordered Spider, Heinie, and three other ringleaders seized up in the rigging; sent the port watch below, and soon had the rest of the crew busy about the ship. The mutiny was over almost as quickly as it had started.

David was encouraged to find both Captain Hunter and Mr. Macy coming around all right, and Mr. Starbuck was soon discovered below decks badly injured, but not killed. He had been attacked by the mutineers, together with Frank, when the two had gone below to disarm Dago Jack. But while Frank had staggered back on deck, the Portuguese had slashed Mr. Starbuck so badly with his knife that the first mate had been unable to move. He was now taken to the cabin which was made into a sick-bay. All the officers were more or less laid up, and Uncle Bob, whose advent on deck had caused a new attack of fever, was still very feeble and ill.

Captain Hunter could hardly believe the story he was told of what had happened.

'The scoundrels, the scoundrels!' he muttered under his breath. 'It's good riddance to bad rubbish, gettin' rid of that murderous Dago Jack. You say young David threw himself on him and then shot him dead? By the great horn spoon! That boy's got spunk. He's a fighter. He saved my life, by gosh! I won't be forgettin' that. Why, he saved the ship!'

XX

HOMEWARD BOUND

The Boat-Steerer

Chapter XX

HOMEWARD BOUND

THE Sea Turtle had been close to the Marquesas on that fearful day of mutiny, and the next morning land was clearly in sight. Captain Hunter thankfully set a course toward shore and soon the ship lay safely anchored in a little harbor.

There she stayed for almost a week, the officers slowly recovering from their injuries while the crew were given frequent shore leave. With Dago Jack awarded a not very sad sea burial, and both Spider and Heinie in irons, there was no more talk of mutiny. Also Frank was right about no one trying to desert while he had a chance for the high lay which the ambergris would bring him. When Captain Hunter ordered the anchor up, every man was aboard ship.

For several weeks the Sea Turtle then cruised off the islands and a few more whales were captured. Everything went well. Mr. Starbuck limped about rather painfully, both Captain Hunter and Frank still had their heads swathed in bandages, but even Uncle Bob was up and about. The forecastle was a far pleasanter place than it had been for a long time, with the mutineers confined by themselves, and, while being so short-handed meant more work for everyone,

the fresh supplies obtained at the Marquesas and better luck
on the whaling grounds caused a marked change in the whole
atmosphere. Finally the time came when the Sea Turtle
was turned homeward, and the sturdy little vessel started
on the long return voyage to New Bedford.

One day a sudden squall blew up. All in an instant the
sun was clouded over, a gust of wind and rain swept down
on the ship, and before the crew could obey Captain Hunter's
order to stand by to take in sail, the canvas was stripped
from the yards. The Sea Turtle scudded before the storm
with bare poles as sea after sea broke over her, carrying off
the starboard whaleboat and sending a torrent of water
below decks. Then as suddenly as it had come upon them,
the squall swept on. The crew were set to the pumps, the
vessel put to her proper course, and new sails brought out.
The flurry and excitement were soon forgotten as the men
worked away to repair the unexpected damage.

Sent aloft to bend on the new sails, David recalled wonderingly those first days at sea when even in the calmest weather
a climb to the yardarms seemed such a perilous journey.
Now it meant nothing to him. He was completely at home in
the ship's rigging and thought condescendingly of that ignorant green hand, that country boy with hayseed still in
his hair, who had come aboard the Sea Turtle more than
two years ago.

He was becoming anxious to get home, however. Going
through the routine work aboard ship, taking his turn at the
masthead and his trick at the wheel, he often recalled his life
on his father's farm. He thought of the long, hot days in
the hayfield, the old swimming hole he passed on his way
home from the far pasture, the pies his mother used to bake.
How long would it be before the Sea Turtle would be warping

into the dock at New Bedford? How soon could he count on seeing his home and his family again?

But there was no hurrying the old whaleship. She was not built for speed. Besides, there were still a few empty oil casks in her hold. Captain Hunter had no idea of pushing his vessel so long as there remained any chance of getting a little more oil. The lookouts were always manned.

As he was leaning over the rail one afternoon, watching the vessel's prow cut through the water and turn up a white furrow in the deep green sea, David was surprised to find Mr. Macy beside him.

'Do you think you could handle a harpoon if we get another chance to lower?'

David's heart leaped. That had long been his dearest wish. If he only got a chance to throw a harpoon, how proudly he could return home! He had not dared to hope for it. He had often handled the heavy irons, getting Frank to tell him how a harpoon should be held and thrown, and twice when a boat had been lowered after porpoises, he had prevailed upon his friend to let him have a try at harpooning them. He had not once succeeded, but the practice had given him some idea of how it should be done. He did not hesitate now.

'Yes, sir,' he answered, 'I think I could.'

As he looked up at Mr. Macy, he recalled another conversation. Leaning over the vessel's side, much as they were now doing, had not the mate asked him some two years ago if he could pull an oar if the boats were lowered after whales? He had made good on that; by graminy, he could make good as a harpooner.

'Well, Captain Hunter thinks you might have a try at it,' Mr. Macy was saying. 'I've seen you working out with an iron. Perhaps you could do it. Anyway, we're short a har-

pooner now that Dago Jack's out of the way. Since you had
something to do with that, maybe you ought to take over
some of his work. If there's a call to lower, report to my
boat.'

Mr. Macy moved away, paying no attention to the boy's
'Yes, sir; thank you, sir.' But David looked after him, with
gratitude and hero-worship in his clear blue eyes. Some day
he'd like to be a whaling officer like Mr. Macy. And here
was his first chance to show what he could do.

After this conversation, David's chief interest was no
longer how soon the Sea Turtle would be rounding Cape
Horn and striking northward up through the Atlantic. He
did not think so often of New Bedford and his father's farm.
He was torn by anxiety lest the vessel reach port without
first sighting another school of whales. His happiest moments were at the masthead and, whenever he was on deck,
he was as likely as not to be perched some place where his
keen eyes could sweep the horizon for the distant spouting
of a spermaceti.

But day after day and week after week went by without
so much as a sign of a whale. The Sea Turtle made her way
across the Pacific, rounded Cape Horn in fair weather, and
headed northward along the South American coast. With
every day the chance of raising whales became smaller. He
was afraid Captain Hunter would give up all hope and order
the try-works overboard, usual sign that the voyage was
ended as far as getting oil was concerned. But until New
Bedford's roofs and steeples were actually in sight, Captain
Hunter had no idea of doing anything like that. The boats
were ready to be lowered any moment.

One quiet afternoon most of the watch were sitting about
on deck lazily dozing in the warm sunshine. David was half

asleep, stretched out by the windlass. Even he was caught napping by the long-drawn-out cry of 'There she blows!'

'Where away?' cried Captain Hunter.

'On the lee beam!' shouted back the lookout. 'She blows! She blows!'

David was the first man at the boat. Usually he waited to get a sight of the spouting whales, to discover how many there were. This time his only idea was to get to his boat. He wanted to be first away; to get his chance to harpoon.

It turned out to be a small school of right whales and soon the boats were lowered and in hot pursuit. Pulling the harpooner's oar, with his eye firmly fixed on the iron lying there ready at hand, the boy was fully as excited as he had been on his first chase. When it became clear that they were catching up on the whales, he waited nervously for the order to stand up.

When it came he sprang up instantly, seized his harpoon, and took his place in the bow with knee braced against the gunwale. He caught a hurried glimpse of the thrashing flukes and glistening back of the whale, and felt suddenly weak and helpless.

'There's his hump!' came the tense command. 'Give it to him! Give it to him!'

David drew back his arm, hesitated for one fearful second, and then with a rush of confidence hurled the iron with all his strength. It sank deep into the animal's side, up to the hitches. The whaleboat pulled up short. David was thrown off his feet, a shower of spray and scalding steam shot over the boat, and a glancing blow from the whale's flukes sent the little craft careening over on one side. For a moment it seemed that all was over with them, but the boat righted itself, and, as the harpooned whale plunged madly ahead, the line began to run out with such speed that blue clouds of smoke rose from the loggerhead.

'Wet the line! Wet the line!' Mr. Macy shouted.

Snatching off his hat he began pouring water over the loggerhead. A few additional turns were taken about it with the line, and then, as the boat flew through the water, David and Mr. Macy perilously exchanged places. The boy found himself in the stern, steering a boat which was fast to a whale he himself had harpooned. Never had he had a more thrilling experience.

The whale dragged them over an hour before Mr. Macy got a chance to hurl his lance. And then it took several darts before the whale began to spout blood. But the kill was made; the whale went into its flurry. David had made good on his first chance as harpooner.

One of the other boats had also killed a whale at this lowering, and two days were spent in cutting-in and trying-out the blubber. It was, however, to be the last time the crew had to go through this hard work. When the last bit of oil had been cooled and stowed away, not an empty barrel was left aboard the Sea Turtle. She was a full ship.

No need now to man the mastheads. No need now to be ready to lower. With his vessel's hold bursting with oil, Captain Hunter was as eager as any member of his crew to get back to New Bedford. The order was given to break up the brick try-works; the long search for oil was over. The voyage had been a success.

They had killed, in all, forty-seven whales; some eighteen hundred barrels of oil were stowed away in the hold. If prices were high, the voyage might net forty thousand dollars, together with what could be obtained for the ambergris. As his share of the profits, his one two-hundred and fiftieth lay, David would earn perhaps one hundred and fifty dollars. Not very much, perhaps, for two and a half years at sea, but it would be the first money the boy had earned, and many a whaleman had come home from an even longer voyage with not half as much to his credit. Little wonder that, from Captain Hunter to David, every man aboard the Sea Turtle cheerfully looked forward to the day when land would be sighted.

The exciting moment when that did happen found David standing with Frank and Uncle Bob at the rail. They had been talking of the voyage, recalling its various incidents and all their exciting adventures.

'Land ho! Land ho!' came the shrill cry from the masthead.

David strained his eyes. At first he could see nothing. Then suddenly he caught sight of it.

'I see it! I see it!' he shouted. 'There's land! Hooray! Hooray!'

He had not noticed that Captain Hunter had come down from the quarterdeck, and jumped involuntarily when he heard his voice right behind him.

'Well, David, yer glad to see land?'

'Yes, sir, I am; I am.'

'I'm not so sorry myself,' Captain Hunter said in a gruff but kindly voice. 'It looks good after a long time at sea.'

He put his hand on David's shoulder.

'You've made good, lad. I'm not forgettin' what you did the time Dago Jack tried to capture the ship. You always got a friend in Obadiah Hunter. What's more, we've made a whaleman out of you. Yes, sir, we made a whaleman out of you.'

He stood silent for a moment.

'We'll be in port a while, then the Sea Turtle will be sailin' after whales again. I'll be with her. That's the way we do, me and my ship, we hunt whales. And I guess I'll be needin' a smart young harpooner on the next voyage. What do you say, lad, do you think you'd like to sign up again?'

Captain Hunter was smiling as David glanced up at him, and the boy's answering smile flashed back immediately. He breathed deeply.

'Thank you, sir,' he said quietly. 'I guess I'd like to, all right.'

THE END

DATE DUE

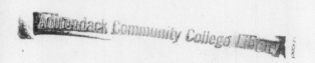